SILENCE IN THE SAGE

Frontier Brides, Book 1

Colleen L. Reece

CHIVERS

British Library Cataloguing in Publication Data available

This Large Print edition published by AudioGO Ltd, Bath, 2012.
Published by arrangement with the Author.

U.K. Hardcover   ISBN   978 1 4458 2608 0
U.K. Softcover   ISBN   978 1 4458 2609 7

Printed and bound in Great Britain by
MPG Books Group Limited

Dear Readers,

I hope you enjoy reading *Silence in the Sage*, the first entry in the FRONTIER BRIDES series, as much as I enjoyed writing it. My parents had a deep love for reading and western history. They passed it on to my brothers and me. One Christmas during hard times Mom splurged and bought Dad twenty Zane Grey books. The $14 gift provided many happy hours reading by kerosene lamp light).

After World War 2 ended and money wasn't so tight, we camped all over the western states and saw places we already knew from Zane Grey's accurate descriptions. Those trips strengthened my desire to write western novels "someday."

"Someday" came years later when, in 1977, I felt called to walk off my government job and write full-time. Now, with six million copies of my 140+ "Books You Can Trust" sold, I marvel. God chose an ordinary logger's daughter to help make the world a better place by providing inspirational reading.

May the FRONTIER BRIDES series bring a smile, a tear, inspiration, and hope to each of you.

In His Service,
Colleen L. Reece

CHAPTER 1

With a mighty pull on the reins and an oath, the burly stagecoach driver slowed his team to a trot, finally halting them square in the middle of the dusty West Texas road.

"What's wrong, Pete?" Gideon Carroll Scott roused from his passenger view of the familiar landscape that hadn't changed in the five years he'd been away.

"C'mon, Gideon, you haven't been gone so long you've forgotten what tricks this cursed country can play on a man, now have you?" Pete cocked his grizzled head to one side. "Hear that?"

Gideon strained his ears but heard nothing. A silence unusual to the stage route remained unbroken by even a bird's cry or rustle of a bunchgrass. Even the normally swaying bluebonnets stood still.

For a heartbeat, Gideon again became the seventeen-year-old about to leave for study in New Orleans, who had experienced this peculiar silence on a final ride with his brother. Cyrus, two years older, had yelled, "Take cover! Silence in the sage like this means a terrible storm is coming." He spurred his horse, and Gideon tore after him, but even the fastest horse couldn't outrun the winds that whipped around the Circle S ranch miles out of *El Paso del Norte,* the Pass of the North.

Gideon exulted in the rising wind and the flying sand, yet common sense and training brought fear as well. Too many men had lost their lives because they couldn't beat the elements.

Now the same stillness pervaded. The scent of gray-green sage intensified with the first stirrings of the wind. Lizards had long since fled to shelter. While the world seemed to wait, Gideon's heart pounded.

"We'll try for the rocks," Pete shouted over the dull roar in the distance. "Hang on." He whipped up the horses. "Giddap, you long-legged, no-good beasts!"

Gideon hastily pulled his head back inside the stagecoach. For a long way, he had ridden on top with Pete, but the rare privacy afforded by being the only coach passenger had been too enticing. He smoothed light brown hair, soon to be sun-streaked from riding and ranch chores, and took a deep breath. The reflection of excitement glowed in his Texas blue-sky eyes, and his lean body swayed with the rocking coach. Would they make the huge pile of windswept rocks before the storm hit? he wondered anxiously.

The clear summer sky darkened. Tiny grains of flying sand heralded gusts of sand-laden wind that flattened the sage and raged behind the lumbering coach. Gideon could barely see Pete's hunched shoulders and pulled-down hat, and the driver's yells blended with the growing wind.

"Made it, by the powers!" Pete drove the team behind the frail shelter provided by the rock pile. The next second, he leaped to the ground, grabbed blankets, and adroitly fastened them over the horses' heads to protect them from the blowing sand. Sweating and trembling, the steeds finally stilled beneath his strong and familiar hands.

With a soft scarf over his mouth and nose, Gideon had burrowed back against the innermost rock by the time Pete staggered toward him. "Here," he called and reached out to guide Pete in the ever-increasing storm.

"Worst thing about these storms is they come without warnin'," Pete complained as he slid his scarf over his eyes. He proceeded to lie flat on his stomach and buried his face in his crossed arms. Gideon followed suit. Flying sand still stung the inch of exposed neck between his shirt collar and low-drawn hat. Good thing he'd firmly resisted dressing in his new clerical suit for his return to San Scipio, the closest town to the Circle S. Uncomfortable but inwardly filled with the same defiant attitude toward the weather he'd had as a boy, Gideon longed to laugh at the storm and howl with the wind. Protected somewhat by the rocks, he and Pete would sensibly wait out the storm and be on their way.

"If only my New Orleans friends could see me now," he muttered. "They'd remind me that West Texas is no place for a brand-new minister!"

"Say somethin'?" Pete grunted.

"Not important." Gideon wouldn't have been able to explain if he'd wanted to. Pete's prejudices against anything except what he called a cursed land (but "wouldn't leave for a million pesos") were legendary.

Gideon sighed. All his persuading hadn't changed his friends' ideas — especially Emily Ann's — that he lived in a barren wasteland. Soft, small, and pretty, Emily Ann had tried to dissuade the young seminary student from his vow to serve in a land that needed to know God as more than a curse. Without conceit, he accepted the fact he could have married Emily Ann if he'd consented to remain in New Orleans.

Give up the rugged Guadalupe Mountains, the Pecos and Rio Grande Rivers, the deep draws that hid stray and stolen cattle, even the blazing summers and frigid winters? Life with Emily Ann and her kind offered little in comparison with home. The Circle S sprawled across a thousand acres that included everything from mountains and canyons to level grazing land.

In vain, Gideon tried to picture Emily Ann's reaction to the huge adobe home built around a courtyard in typical Mexican style. Thick walls kept out both heat and cold but kept in comfort and warmth. Bright blankets and dark polished wood, carefully tended flowers, and colorful desert paintings contrasted sharply with the restored homes in New Orleans that had escaped the devastation of the War Between the States. Gideon sometimes wondered if Emily Ann ever thought of the hardship the South had experienced. Her family had spirited her away at the first sign of trouble, and although she plaintively complained of "those cold and uncarin' Yankees," he knew she had reveled in the attention received while staying in the North. Once, she stroked the rich damask of the portieres and said, "To think that *Yankees* came down here and tried to tell us how to live!" Her silvery laughter grated on Gideon's nerves, and he bit his lip to keep from reminding her that few Southerners had been able to rebuild in the way of her wealthy family.

Gideon shook his sand-laden shoulders. San Scipio and the Circle S would seem unbearably crude to a young woman like Emily Ann. He buried his face deeper in his arms, wishing the storm would stop its roaring and go on its way. Yet wasn't this time of waiting exactly what he had felt he needed before reaching home? More than miles lay between the ranch and Louisiana. With each *clip-clop* of the horses' steady gait, Gideon became less the student and more the rangeman he had once been. At times he had to reach into his satchel and feel the reassuring crackle of his rolled diploma, the only tangible evidence that proclaimed he had completed his ministerial studies.

Now his fingers involuntarily crept to his vest pocket. Even his father would find no fault with the record his younger son had made. A clipping from a New Orleans newspaper already had creases from being unfolded and refolded. The late nights and devotion to study that enraged Emily Ann had put Gideon at the top of his class. Surely Elijah Scott would take his love-blind gaze from Cyrus at least long enough to acknowledge his achievement.

Don't count on it, his inner voice counseled. *Lige Scott is a great rancher, a staunch follower of the Almighty — according to what he thinks — but this love for the firstborn son is only rivaled by that of Old Testament patriarchs. In his opinion, Cyrus can do no wrong.*

Once when Gideon was a child, his mother, Naomi, tried to explain his father's feelings. "We were married for so long before we had children, Lige wondered if God were punishing him for something — don't ask me what." Her blue eyes so like Gideon's turned dreamy. "It is hard to be such a strong and powerful man like your father and yet not be able to control his own son."

"I'm his son, too," Gideon had piped in his treble voice.

"I know. So does he, when he stops to remember. We must accept him the way he is, Gideon." Naomi turned and gazed out the window. "It took strength to leave everything we knew and come to Texas after it became a state in 1845. The way was hard. Many in our party didn't make it. Every death diminished Lige, for his enthusiasm had been the driving force that encouraged friends to make the journey with us. Once we got here, he worked hard, harder than any one man should work. He stood by my bedside when Cyrus was born and watched us both nearly die. Is it any wonder he cannot see faults in the son who finally came from God?"

"But, Mother, you went through all that, too," the youthful Gideon protested. "The long trail, the hard work."

"It is different for a woman," Naomi gently said. A light her son would never forget shone in her eyes. "Women are helpmeets, companions, and strengtheners to their men. I pray that one day God will send to you a strong, true wife."

"She must be like you," Gideon sturdily maintained.

His mother ruffled the sun-streaked hair and laughed. "We hope she is much better," she teased. "Now, get about your studies. Even though he says little and expects much, your father is proud of the way you grasp learning. Besides, it will be many years before you need think of taking a wife!"

Gideon coughed against the closeness of

the scarf across his face, then chuckled to himself. He could imagine the look on his mother's face if Emily Ann had been willing to visit Texas. The chuckle faded. Perhaps the response from the child that his future wife must be like Naomi had secretly built up resistance to Emily Ann.

Would the storm never end? Who could tell whether minutes had turned to hours in this poorly sheltered spot? Gideon forced himself to look again to the past to avoid the miserable present.

Born in El Paso in May 1852, Gideon was just nine years old when Texas seceded from the Union and joined the Confederate States of America in 1861. Yet those days remained clear in his mind. He had asked Cyrus, "How can part of a country just cut itself off? Isn't that like my fingers saying they won't be part of my body?"

Eleven-year-old Cyrus had ignored the question. "Father doesn't want to talk about it. He says a lot of trouble can come from what's happening." For once the careless, daring boy was cowed. "I heard him talking with Mother. He says there is going to be war."

"You mean people killing each other, like in our books?" Gideon jerked up straight. "But we're going to feel the same way."

15

The war years hadn't changed life drastically on the Circle S. Season followed season. Stock had to be rounded up and driven to market. Chores kept needing to be done. Yet long after the fighting ended and Congress readmitted Texas to the Union in 1870, two years after the elder Scott's native Louisiana again became part of the Union, Gideon remembered the lines that etched themselves in his father's face and aged him.

During those years, Cyrus and Gideon entered early manhood. Cyrus laughed at the idea of wanting to learn more than he already knew from books. He rode like a burr in the saddle; roped, hunted, and tracked like an Indian; gambled and drank; and yet managed to keep his father unaware of his grosser habits. Gideon sometimes wondered how Lige could fail to see the marks of debauchery when Cyrus returned from a spree with a story of being holed up through a storm or off herding cattle. Bitterly, the younger son reminded himself again and again of his father's well-known blind spot. Years of standing in Cyrus's shadow had produced a certain callousness, but his tender heart still longed for a father's approval.

Gideon's fifteenth birthday seemed a

welcome harbinger, as shortly afterward a hardened-to-the-saddle traveling minister arrived in San Scipio. Never had the inhabitants of the little western town heard the Word of God preached with such power and passion. The few services made an indelible mark on a boy who had known about God since the cradle. At fifteen, Gideon came to know God and His plan of salvation through His Only Son, Jesus, as the most challenging, exciting story life offers. He said nothing to his family, but the next weeks and months of riding gave him opportunity to let the knowledge of God's goodness sink deep into his soul. On his sixteenth birthday, he dug fingernails into his callused palms, stood square in his worn boots, and told his parents, "I want to be a minister."

The tornado he expected failed to come. To Gideon's amazement, the nearest to an expression of approval Lige had ever given his son came to the seamed face. "Do you feel the Almighty is behind this, or are you just looking for a way to get off the Circle S?" Lige asked quickly but thoughtfully. A flush of pleasure and determination arose in Gideon's anxious heart.

He straightened to his full five-foot, ten-inch height, his keen blue glance never wavering. "I have to tell others what God did for all of us."

"Then go to it, Son." Lige's mighty hand crushed his son's in a grip that would have broken the bones of a lesser young man. "I need your help for a time, but I give my word. On your seventeenth birthday, if you still feel this is what God wants of you, we'll send you to New Orleans. There are still some distant relatives there, a few of whom are rebuilding. You'll be welcome." A wry smile crossed his face. "More than welcome. You'll naturally pay your way, and the money will help them."

True to his word, Gideon embarked on his new life the day he turned seventeen. To his amazement, Cyrus traveled with him. Only the night before, he confessed that he hankered to see New Orleans for himself and aimed to find a pretty little filly to bring home, if there was one who had the nerve to tackle Texas and take him on.

After some protest, Lige rolled his big eyes and agreed to the change in plans. "I reckon we can get along without you the rest of this spring and through the summer," he admitted. "Mind you, be back by fall roundup, though." His crisp order couldn't hide the pride he carried for his older son, who stood an inch taller and outweighed the stripling Gideon by fifteen pounds.

While Gideon settled into the studies that would give him the background Lige insisted he have "to be not just a parson, but a *good* one," Cyrus hit New Orleans like a cannonball. In spite of lodging with the same relatives, the brothers seldom saw each other. Spring bloomed into summer, and Cyrus played at being New Orleans's most eligible bachelor. Gideon dove into his books like a man starving for knowledge. The rare occasions when their paths crossed offered little opportunity to share more than greetings.

Suddenly Cyrus grew restless. "Can't stand this heat," he told his brother and mopped his brow. "At least in Texas when it's hot, you aren't so dripping wet all the time. Besides, I'm sick of the scent of oleander." He grinned his devil-may-care grin and added, "I'll take trail dust and the smell of sage anytime."

Instead of staying until fall, Cyrus awakened Gideon one sweltering mid-August night. Eyes red and breath foul with the fumes of brandy, he muttered, "Going home. Nothing worth staying for here," and then he lurched out. By the time Gideon came fully awake to dress and reach his brother's room, Cyrus lay passed out on his bed.

Gideon felt torn between love and disgust. Why couldn't Cyrus see what he was doing to himself? Why didn't he accept Jesus and find excitement in following Him instead of seeking it in gambling halls and who knew what other places? For a moment, he wanted to shake some sense into Cyrus, but he finally went back to bed. He regretted his decision the next morning when he went to Cyrus's room, now laid bare of all clothing and belongings.

Weeks later, Naomi wrote that Cyrus had come home "without the filly he hoped to rope" and rather quiet. Gideon suspected his brother had tarried along the way to rid himself of the marks of dissipation accumulated during his binge in New Orleans.

"Gideon?" Pete's voice interrupted his companion's reverie. "You still alive in there?" A rough hand shook his shoulder, and sand cascaded off Gideon's hat, shirt, and vest. He sat up and stamped his feet, tingling from the movement after their cramped position during the storm.

"Passed on by, didn't it?" Gideon jerked the scarf off his face and watched Pete busy himself with unmasking the team. "Arghh! Feel like I rolled in a sandbank."

"Better be thankin' that God of yours we ain't plumb smothered." Pete's weather-split lips opened in a grin. He finished with the horses, which stamped much as the men had done, obviously glad to rid themselves of their burden of sand.

Pete tossed a canteen to Gideon, then gave each of the horses water in his big, cupped hand. "Drink up. There's enough to get us to San Scipio, and we'll water down good there."

Curious at the comment about thanking God, Gideon replied, "I'll ride the rest of the way on top."

Pete just grunted, but when they got back on the road and headed through the sage toward San Scipio and home, Gideon asked, "Pete, why'd you say that, I mean, about being thankful?"

"Think preachers are the only ones who know God's ridin' the trails and watchin' over folks?" Pete shot back, then slapped the horses with the reins. "Giddap." He swallowed some choice name for the animals and added, "I know what you're thinkin'. I ain't much, and I don't claim to be nothin' but what I am, an ornery, miserable stagecoach driver. But I reckon it's ungrateful not to be glad the Almighty's on the job."

A thrill went through Gideon. *Could he encourage the seed of faith in Pete's tough old heart?* "You know the Almighty cared enough about *all of us,*" he emphasized the words, "to send His Son to die for us."

"Pretty big of Him." But Pete's voice discouraged further comment, and he gruffly added, "Save your preachin', Boy. It ain't goin' to be easy to start out in your home range." He sent a sharp glance at his passenger. "How come you didn't just stay in New Orleans? Plenty of churches there, ain't they?"

"That's why, Pete," Gideon quietly said. "San Scipio doesn't have even one, and the way I figure it, home folks have just as much right to hear the gospel as city folks." He stared unseeingly at the road ahead. "I know lots of them will think I'm just a kid. I guess I am!" He laughed, and some of his melancholy left. "Not that I'm comparing myself, but the Bible tells about a whole lot of people who spoke for the Lord when they were even younger than I. Jesus talked with the priests in the temple when He was only twelve. I'm ten years older than that."

"Didja do some preachin' for practice back there?" Pete asked. "Were you scared?"

"Scareder than the time I tangled with a polecat and had to go home and face my father," Gideon confessed.

Pete threw his head back and roared.

"Son, you're gonna be all right. Just keep rememberin' who it is you're doin' this for and don't pay no mind to those who give you, uh, fits." He quickly changed the subject. "Where you goin' to start in preachin'?"

Gideon wondered at the gleam in Pete's eye but only said, "Mother wrote that Father had made some kind of arrangement for a building." His straight brows drew together. "My dream is to have a real church in San Scipio someday."

"Hmm." Pete swung the horses successfully around a bend and motioned with his whip handle. "There it is."

From their vantage point on the hill, they could see into the sleepy town of San Scipio, nestled between the rises. One long, dusty street boasted a few weathered buildings and a hitching rail, where a few lazy horses were tethered. Shade trees offered some protection from the blazing sun, and back from the main thoroughfare, several homes of varying ages and styles stood closed against the afternoon heat.

" 'Pears mighty quiet," Pete mumbled and urged the horses into a trot toward the general store, which served as a stage stop.

Why should the sleepy village cause a

sense of foreboding, Gideon wondered. Or was it just the unexpected silence?

CHAPTER 2

The arrival of the stage seemed to wave a magic wand that brought the drowsy hamlet of San Scipio back to life. Pete threw down the mail sack, and Gideon leaped to the ground.

"Hyar!" A heavy hand fell on his shoulder.

Gideon spun around in obedience to the touch and voice of authority he hadn't known in five years. Except for a few more lines in his weather-beaten face and the glimmer of a smile so rare his younger son could count on his fingers the times he'd seen it, Lige Scott stood tall, strong, and unchanged. "Welcome home, Son."

The young minister's vision blurred. Could the approval in Lige's voice and face really be for him? He glanced around. "Mother? Cyrus?" His keen gaze caught the darkening of Lige's face.

"At the ranch. Your mother's busy killing the fatted calf."

Strange that the same parable that ran through Gideon's mind fell from Lige's lips. "And Cyrus?"

"Rounding up strays." Lige threw his massive head back, and the Scott blue eyes flashed. With a visible effort, he put aside whatever was troubling him. "I brought the wagon. Figured you'd have a lot of things that needed fetching to the Circle S."

Strangely relieved of the tension he didn't understand, Gideon laughed, and its clear, ringing sound brought an answering chuckle from Pete, who had held back from greeting Lige. "Thought for sure we'd sink when we forded the stream," he joshed as he helped the other two transfer trunks and nailed wooden boxes of books from the stage to the wagon. But when Lige and Gideon climbed into the wagon and the older man took the reins, Pete called, "Don't fergit who you're workin' for."

The horses swung into a rhythmic beat before Lige demanded, "What was Pete talking about?" Lige's long years on the range hadn't quite erased his superior feelings toward his less polished neighbors.

"Pete didn't mean anything." Gideon hated himself for his placating tone, but he couldn't help falling back into the same pattern of behavior he'd used as a child to help his mother keep peace in the family. "He was just reminding me that God's my new boss."

"Huh." The grunt could have meant anything.

Gideon glanced from Lige to the road they were taking. "Why, this isn't the way to the ranch."

"Nope." Lige skillfully turned the team to the left at the end of the main street. To Gideon's amazement, he drove toward the road that wound weary miles to El Paso instead of the beaten track toward the Circle S. A quick swing to the left again, and Lige pulled in the horses. "Well, how do you like it?"

Gideon stared, closed his eyes, and blinked and stared again.

"Cat got your tongue? I asked how you like it." Lige flicked a fly off his forehead and pointed with a long, work-worn finger to a brand-new log building sitting back from the road on a little rise. "We hauled logs a lot of miles to build this, so you'd better appreciate it."

His father's grim warning lit a bonfire in Gideon's brain. "It's perfect." He scanned the building that bravely sat in its sagebrush and mesquite surroundings. Large enough to house all of San Scipio and those who ranched around it, the little wilderness church nonetheless remained small enough to be cozy.

"Dad —" Gideon couldn't go on. He barely heard his own voice using the informal name for the first time.

"I said I'd find a place for you to preach, didn't I?" Lige sounded gruffer than ever. "Well, are you going to sit there like a coyote on a rock or get down and go in?"

Gideon jumped from the wagon and walked through a welter of desert flowers someone had lovingly planted on both sides of the wide, dusty track to the door of the church. Sunflowers and bluebonnets were still damp from a recent watering; the hard clay soil around them lay dry and cracked in places. Blue mountains loomed miles away, yet in the clear air, they looked close enough to reach in minutes.

Gideon's heart swelled. He reached for the door and lifted the latch. Late afternoon sun streamed through windows that must have been hauled in from El Paso. The scent of freshly sawed wood crept into his nostrils. Peace and humility filled his soul. The silence inside the simple building bore evidence of his father's love and the devotion of a town that waited for the gospel of Jesus Christ. Young and inexperienced, could he be worthy of that devotion, worthy of his Lord?

"Well?" Lige's impatient reminder that he waited for an answer whirled Gideon around to face his father.

"It's more beautiful than any church or cathedral I saw while I was gone." Words came faster than tumbleweeds before a wind. "All those churches and cathedrals I saw when you had me visit friends instead of coming home for holidays — why —" He choked off, and his eyes stung. "I wouldn't trade this church for all of those others put together! I'm home. *Home.*"

"Good thing." Lige frowned and turned on his heel. "We'll be dedicating this church come Sunday." He looked back over his shoulder. "Better have a rip-snorting sermon. Folks around here don't want mush." He strode out, his footsteps heavy on the hand-smoothed board floor.

Gideon smothered a laugh. Rip-snorting sermons weren't exactly what he had practiced, but if that's what San Scipio wanted, he couldn't find a better source than the Bible! He looked around the silent, waiting church once more. For the second time, a feeling of unease touched him. The church held everything he could have dreamed of and more. Indeed, he'd supposed his first

29

services would be in some abandoned building or barn. There appeared to be no earthly reason that all was not well. Perhaps the new wrinkles in his father's face had disturbed him or the set of his jaw when he said Cyrus had gone to round up strays. Gideon sighed and carefully closed the door of the new church behind him.

The steady *clip-clop* of the horses' hooves ate up the distance between San Scipio and the Circle S. For as long as Gideon could remember, his father had always stopped the horses for a breather on top of the mesa that sloped steeply above the ranch. Today Gideon was off the wagon seat even before the horses completely stopped. A poignant feeling of never having been away assaulted him. Here he had ridden with Cyrus a hundred times. Here he had reined in the horses on the few solitary trips he made to San Scipio for supplies. A lone eagle winged high above in perfect harmony with the vast wilderness. Below, half hidden by cottonwoods planted when Lige and Naomi first acquired the small piece of land that eventually grew into the present spread, the red-tiled roof and foot-thick cream walls of the house invited weary travelers. Gideon couldn't remember a time that cowboys and cattlemen hadn't been welcome at the

Circle S.

"Your mother'll be waiting," Lige reminded, and Gideon sprang back to the wagon.

"Too bad your brother isn't here." The corners of Lige's mouth turned down, and he scowled. Again Gideon had the feeling all wasn't right between father and son.

Thoughtfully, Gideon tried to turn away Lige's attention. "Coming home has taught me one thing. I never want to live anywhere else. I'll be satisfied if the good Lord provides me with a wife and kids and the chance to live here until I die."

The rustle of yellowed grass beside the wagon track and the scream of the eagle sent a chill down his spine. He sought the Lord in a silent prayer. *Dear God, when things are as near perfect as they ever will be again, please take away this awful sense that something is going to happen.*

When they descended from the mesa and drove up to the corral, Gideon felt prepared to greet his mother, who flew from the ranch house as if pursued by mountain lions. Her brown hair had streaks of gray that hadn't been there when he left, but Gideon noted her slender body hadn't changed. Neither had the blue of her eyes.

"My son." She clasped him close, then

held him off to take measure with one swift glance. Gideon felt on trial for the years he had been gone and actually heaved a sigh of relief when she softly whispered, "It is well. You have kept the faith." With the lightning change of mood he knew so well, she inquired, "And how do you like your father's surprise?"

Gideon thought of the perfect church waiting for his return. "Nothing could have pleased me more." He cautiously turned to make sure Lige had taken the team and wagon on to the barn before adding in a low voice, "For the first time in my whole life, I feel Fa— Dad is proud of me."

"More than you know, especially since —"

Lige's hail stilled any confidences she might have shared. "Is Cyrus back?"

"Just in." Naomi bit her lip, and Gideon saw the familiar pleading in her suddenly serious face. Lige might deny and refuse to accept that his first-born son fell short of perfection but not Naomi. Still, for her husband's sake, she strove for harmony by cushioning the clashes that periodically came.

"What's all the shouting about?" a lazy voice drawled from the wide, covered roof extension that made a cool porch. Cyrus lounged against one side of an arched support. "Well, little brother, you ready to save everyone's souls?"

Lige growled deep in his throat as Cyrus tossed a half-smoked brown-paper cigarette to the earth and ground it with his boot heel. "Sorry, Dad. Just have to make sure Gideon remembers he's no angel, even if he is going to proclaim the good news."

Gideon hated the sarcasm that had always reduced him to a tongue-tied fool. This time he found his voice. "I never claimed to be an angel. You know that."

"Good thing." Cyrus's eyes gleamed with mischief as he gripped his brother's hand, and Gideon gave back as hearty a squeeze as he received. "Well! This boy's no tender-foot, even if he has been living soft in the city."

"Did you find any strays?" Lige boomed, his ox-eyed gaze firmly on Cyrus.

"Some. Not as many as I expected." Cyrus shrugged. "My horse threw a shoe, and I had to come back in sooner than I planned."

"Get it fixed, and get back out into the canyons tomorrow," Lige dictated.

A wave of red ran from Cyrus's shirt collar up to his uneven hairline. "Yes, Sir!" He saluted smartly, and Gideon held his breath, but before his father could roar, Cyrus threw an arm around his brother. "Rosa and Carmelita have been cooking for days. Let's eat." He grinned at Lige the way Gideon never could do, and a reluctant smile softened their father's features.

"Give us time to wash," the head of the household ordered. "Then bring on the feast."

An hour later, Gideon sat back with a sigh of repletion. The remains of his homecoming dinner lay before him. Tamales, enchiladas, chicken, a half-dozen kinds of fruits and vegetables from the garden, and a glistening chocolate cake had been reduced to crumbs. "I haven't eaten like this since I left," he murmured.

"Temperance in all things, Brother Gideon." Cyrus pulled his face into a sanctimonious smirk. "It won't do for your congregation to know you are a glutton."

In the wave of laughter from family and servants alike, Gideon wondered how he could ever have had qualms about his return to San Scipio and the Circle S.

Not satisfied with his needling, Cyrus continued. "So, what is your text for Sunday, Brother Gideon?"

An unexplainable impulse caused him to retort, "Perhaps I'll use Cain's question, 'Am I my brother's keeper?' Genesis 4:9," he added in the spirit of fun.

A cannonball exploding in the middle of the long table couldn't have produced more devastation. Cyrus leaped to his feet, anger distorting his features. "Just what do you mean?" He glared at his brother much as Cain must have done to the ill-fated Abel. "Don't think that becoming a parson is going to make you anything except what you are, the *younger* brother." Rage tore away every shred of control. "I'll have no mealy-mouthed, holier-than-thou snob of a brother bossing me around!"

"I didn't mean —" Gideon couldn't believe the ugliness of his brother's discourse.

"Sit down, Cyrus," Lige commanded. He stared at Gideon. "I'll have no such talk at the table or anywhere else on this ranch. As Cyrus says, being a preacher gives you no right to make remarks about your brother."

Gideon started to protest but caught the patient and resigned shake of his mother's head and subsided, feeling the pain of injustice from Lige's remarks. *Nothing had really changed.* It didn't matter that his father had built a church. When it came to taking sides, Lige Scott would never uphold the younger brother over the elder.

So much for coming home. Perhaps Emily Ann and the others had been right when they said he should have accepted a church somewhere other than in San Scipio. Yet, as he'd told Pete, who needed Jesus more than persons like Cyrus? Jesus clearly taught He came to heal the spiritually sick, not those already in His service.

That night when all had retired and Gideon restlessly moved around his rooms, he wondered. Even his pleasure at discovering Mother had enlarged his former bedroom and cleared out rooms on either side to provide a study and sitting room dwindled at the memory of the supper table scene. As he stood for a long time looking at the brilliant, low-hanging stars in the midnight blue Texas sky, he realized there had to be more behind Cyrus's reaction than not being able to accept joking. In the past, he'd delighted in the few times when Gideon managed to get ahead of him.

As if conjured up by thinking about him, a heavy knock brought Gideon to the door.

"May I come in?" Cyrus's bold gaze took in the refurbished rooms. He raised one eyebrow. "Some accommodations. Personally, all I need or want is a place to sleep." His tone abruptly changed from indolence to vigilance. "I want to know why you said what you did at supper." He stood crouched as if posed to spring.

36

"First thing that popped into my mind," Gideon frankly told him, but a warning went off in his mind. *Cyrus must have some secret to seek me out like this.*

Cyrus relaxed. The smile that could charm a rattlesnake into retreating replaced the watchful gaze. "Sorry." He half closed his eyes again in the habit he had that hid any expression from others. "Like I said, I just don't want you lording it over me." He laughed. "Get it? *Lord*ing over me, although God knows, sometimes I could use a trail-mate like Him, if He's everything Dad and Mother and you think He is." He gave Gideon no opportunity to reply. "If He puts up with me long enough, who knows? I might shock Him and everyone — me included — by asking Him to ride with me." The next moment, he crossed the room in long strides, his spurs clinking musically. "I'm off for a night ride. Want to come?"

Gideon's irritation melted. "Give me five minutes," Gideon told him. He threw on riding clothes and stole out after his brother in the starlight. He felt like a kid again, when he and Cyrus were supposed to be sleeping but went riding instead.

The cool night wind and the exhilaration of riding in the open country blew cobwebs from Gideon's brain and doubt from his heart. All of his love for Cyrus returned, along with an even deeper love for his brother's soul. He might have spilled out the first Scripture that came to mind, but how true it was. Ever since he first accepted Jesus, he had longed above all for Cyrus to do the same. He *was* his brother's keeper. But the night sky and the feeling God lingered close opened his heart to an enlarged truth: Every follower of the lowly Nazarene assumes keepership of all others who need to know Him. The same surety that caused him to announce on his sixteenth birthday that he must spread the gospel of Jesus Christ settled into his soul more deeply than ever.

Before they reached home, Cyrus halted his mount. He waited for his brother to pull up beside him, then addressed him in a low voice. "Gideon, no matter what happens, you'd never go back on me, would you?"

The friendly night had turned menacing. "Of course not." Gideon tried to see Cyrus's expression, but shadows and his low-pulled hat effectively camouflaged his face.

"And you'd forgive me? Seventy times seven?"

"What's this all about?" Gideon demanded sharply. His very soul chilled at some hidden meaning.

"Seventy times seven?" Cyrus repeated, then spurred his horse into a magnificent leap. "Never mind, Kid. Just testing you . . ." Cyrus's racing figure was swallowed up by the darkness.

Gideon slowly followed. Something about Cyrus frightened him. What had his brother been up to? Why should he ask such questions, request such a promise, then ride away before Gideon could answer? He had no more answers when he rubbed down his horse and slipped back into his bed.

The next morning Cyrus had returned to his old teasing self, wanting to know if "the parson" had time to help round up strays or if he planned to sleep all morning and practice his sermon the rest of the day.

Relieved but wary, Gideon rolled out, stowed away an enormous breakfast, and spent the day in the saddle. He came home stiff, sore, and convinced he'd better take it a little easier until he got his old skills back. The next day he settled with a Bible and writing materials and began making notes for the dedication sermon. How could he impress on his neighbors that his youth meant nothing, that the message he bore remained unchanged and unlimited despite the frailties of the messenger who carried it? Time spent on his knees paid off, and over the next several days, Gideon successfully balanced study, preparation, and range riding. Serving his "parish" would entail miles of hard riding to obscure dwellings; he rejoiced when he discovered he no longer felt stiff.

On Saturday night, Cyrus headed for town after being turned down by Gideon, who refused to accompany him. "Yeah, I guess it wouldn't look too good for a preacher to be part of a San Scipio Saturday night," Cyrus admitted. But he didn't heed his brother's pleas for him to stay home, either.

"Will you be there tomorrow?" Gideon asked wistfully.

Cyrus swung to the saddle. "Think I'd miss it? It's going to be better than the entertainment Blackie gets for the Missing Spur."

"I hope so." Gideon shuddered. The Missing Spur Saloon had a reputation for the so-called entertainment offered to its patrons. "How can you stand it?" he blurted out. "Why don't you find yourself a nice girl, instead of hanging around those —"

"Mind your own affairs, Parson." Cyrus's blue eyes turned icy. "If Dad asks where I am, tell him I rode into town to get a new bridle. It's true enough." He pointed to the patched-together job he'd done on his bridle and laughed mockingly. "You never would lie for me, so I won't ask you to. Just keep your lip buttoned about what you may or may not know." His horse impatiently danced, and the next instant, the two vanished except for a dust cloud kicked up behind them.

Gideon disconsolately headed for his room. Although his sermon still needed a few touches, once inside, he stood for a long moment by his deep-set window, watching the wagon track toward San Scipio and praying that somehow God would soften Cyrus's heart.

At last he went to his desk and forced himself to put personal troubles aside, losing himself in the truth of the Scriptures. For hours he considered, rejected, and, in spite of his best efforts, listened for the neigh of a horse, the jingle of spurs, or the soft footsteps that would signal Cyrus had returned.

Darkness paled. Dawn stole over the distant mountains. Gideon awakened from the uncomfortable position where he'd fallen asleep with his head on his crossed arms at the desk. Could Cyrus have sneaked in without him hearing?

In stockinged feet so as not to rouse his parents, the young minister slipped across his room, down the hall, and into Cyrus's bedroom. Yet Gideon's fingers trembled as he pushed open the door and stepped inside.

The room lay empty. The bed, neatly made.

CHAPTER 3

For a long time Gideon stood in the empty room and stared at his brother's unwrinkled bed. Disappointment and the nagging worry something had gone wrong swept over him. Even back in his own rooms, Gideon lay awake, wondering why Cyrus hadn't come home. He had promised not to miss the dedication of the little church and his brother's first sermon in San Scipio.

Gideon found himself defending Cyrus as he had always done. *Maybe when he reached town, his horse went lame and he stayed with friends,* he thought hopefully. Clinging to the thought of what meager comfort it offered, the troubled young minister finally managed to sleep for a few hours. He opened his eyes to a glorious summer Sunday morning and a laugh that sent relief surging through him.

"Cyrus!" Gideon tumbled into his clothes and raced to the courtyard, bright with flowers and shaded by carefully tended trees.

"Well, Parson, is your sermon ready?" Cyrus stood up from teasing a small lizard and turned his brilliant blue gaze toward Gideon.

"Ready as it will ever be." Gideon thought of the hours of prayerful study he had put into that sermon. "Glad to see you made it home. I was beginning to wonder if —"

"Shh." Cyrus furtively looked at the house, then back at his brother. "I'm sorry, but I won't be able to hear your preaching after all."

Gideon's spirits dropped. "Why not?" He stared at his brother, noting the honest regret in Cyrus's face, the misery in his eyes.

"I got word in town that —" Cyrus swallowed and shrugged. "It doesn't matter. I'm riding out as soon as the rest of you leave for church." His fingers crept to his breast pocket. Gideon could see the ragged edge of an opened letter before Cyrus stuffed it deeper in his pocket.

"When will you be back?"

"Maybe never." The somber voice stayed low, barely discernible.

"You can't mean that!" Gideon burst out. "It will kill Father. If you're in trouble, say so. You know we'll stand behind you."

Cyrus's lips twisted, then set in a grim, uncompromising line. "Not this time." He raised his voice and gave Gideon a warning look. "Well, Father, today is a proud day for the Scotts, isn't it?"

Yet Gideon saw the strong face crumple for a moment before Cyrus averted his face from Lige Scott's beaming glance. His heart felt like a cannonball in his chest. *I must find a chance to talk with Cyrus before leaving for San Scipio!*

His brother proved more clever than he. After he finished breakfast, Cyrus looked at the big clock that had traveled west with the older Scotts and then made an announcement. "Instead of riding in the buggy with you, I'll take my horse, and then I can head for El Paso after church. Talk around town is that one of the ranchers there is selling out and going back East. Maybe I can pick up a few head of prime horses."

"Not on the Sabbath," Lige ordered. "Stay in town and see the horses tomorrow."

"I reckon it won't hurt just to look at them on the Sabbath, will it?" Cyrus assumed an air of injured innocence. "The buying part can wait." He strode out without waiting for a reply.

After excusing himself, Gideon followed Cyrus outside. At the corral, Cyrus had already uncoiled his rope to lasso the horse he wanted. "Cyrus, *don't go,*" Gideon pleaded, out of breath from chasing him.

"I have to." The rope drooped from his fingers. "I'll ride out of sight, then when you're gone, I'll come back for a few belongings."

"I don't understand," Gideon cried.

"I hope to God you never do." The lariat sang and expertly dropped around a big bay's neck. Before Gideon could think of a way to stop Cyrus, his brother had saddled the bay, mounted, and ridden off with a mocking farewell wave. Shaken, Gideon wondered how he could go ahead and preach just a few hours later. He retraced his steps to the house, but instead of joining his parents, he went to his room, knelt by the bed, and stayed there for a long time, unable to pray.

When the Scotts arrived in a churchyard crowded with horses, buggies, wagons, and people on foot, a most irreverent cheer arose. A startled Gideon observed Lige's broad shoulders held straight and proud and Naomi's shy smile. Now that the day for which she'd waited so long had arrived, it seemed the most natural thing in the world to be helped down from the buggy seat and ushered into a sweet-smelling church. The absence of piano and organ did not discourage the lusty a cappella singing of familiar hymns. In this first service ever held in San Scipio in a church, ranchers and merchants, women and children raised their voices in harmony and song that lifted even Gideon's disturbed heart.

Then it was time. Clutching the pages he'd labored over so long, Gideon Carroll Scott stepped to the hand-hewn pulpit. As he looked at the first carefully written paragraph of his sermon, the words swam before him. Paralyzing fear such as he'd never known constricted his throat. To hide it, he quickly bowed his head and shot upward a frantic, desperate prayer for help. When the rustling of the congregation stilled, his mind stopped reeling. He opened his eyes and looked at the sermon, then deliberately laid it aside.

"Friends." Gideon paused and looked from one side of the packed church to the other, from front to back. Women in their best dresses held children on their laps. Men sat straight and waiting beside them. Young people eyed one another from the protection of their families. Many had grown so much in the time Gideon had been away, he could only place them by their proximity to the families he knew. Unfamiliar faces stood out like whitecaps in the gulf of waiting souls.

"Friends," he said again, "I had prepared a special sermon that seemed to be in keeping with this significant day." He held up the pages. "I can't give this sermon, at least not today. I feel that Almighty God simply wants me to share with you what He and His Son, Jesus Christ, have done for me."

Warming to the subject, Gideon told in the simplest terms possible how as a fifteen-year-old boy he had invited Jesus into his heart. Something in the way he spoke kept the congregation's attention riveted on him. Babies fell asleep in their mothers' arms. Children listened in wonder. Young and old responded to the Holy Spirit that had prompted Gideon to forsake fancy preaching and merely testify.

He went on to say how he came to know the only thing he wanted to do in life was to help others find Christ, as the traveling minister had done for him. He touched lightly on the years in New Orleans of study and preparation amid the Reconstruction efforts. He said nothing of those who wooed him, who predicted obscurity and waste in a life given to a tiny West Texas town. Instead, the great longing for his friends and neighbors to meet, know, and love the

Lord rang in every word. Gideon could feel the rush of caring and ended by saying, "Not one of us can save ourselves. God in His goodness offers the only plan of salvation the world ever has known or ever will know. Will you open your hearts to His Son?"

He sat down, drained yet exultant. Here and there, faces made hard from years in a raw land trembled with emotion as tears spilled down weathered cheeks. An untrained but harmonious quartet sang the beautiful hymn "Faith of Our Fathers." A short dedicatory prayer followed, and Gideon's trial by fire ended. Handshakes that ranged from the tentative touch of the elderly to staunch grips by mighty men warmed the new preacher. Yet the knowledge that the one he most longed to bring to Jesus even now rode alone and lonely lay heavily on him. So did the guilt of carrying that knowledge.

Although Lige and Naomi didn't think anything about it when Cyrus failed to come home by Wednesday, Lige grumbled because Cyrus had missed the sermon. "Wouldn't have hurt him, and common courtesy demanded he be there," he boomed in his big voice more than once. His brow furrowed until the lines looked even deeper. "Sometimes I wish Cyrus were more like —" He broke off, as if unwilling to express even hesitant disloyalty to his firstborn.

The younger brother's heart pounded at the implied approval, but when Cyrus hadn't returned by Saturday, Gideon knew a crisis was fast approaching. Should he tell Lige the little he knew? Gideon's troubled mind queried. All he really knew was that a certain letter had reached Cyrus that evidently alarmed him into vanishing. Besides, deep in his heart, Gideon couldn't and wouldn't accept Cyrus's desertion. In spite of his faults, Cyrus loved the Circle S and had been branding calves with the S brand shortly after he learned to ride. Gideon had helped when he got old enough, but never had his heart been in it. Always, books and learning and what lay outside his own way of life lured him away from the range.

At supper Saturday evening, Lige turned to Gideon. "Do you know anything about your brother?"

The analogy of Cain and Abel returned: The Lord had inquired of Cain concerning his brother Abel's whereabouts. Unlike Cain, Gideon did not lie when he said he didn't know. He felt compelled to add, "He seemed, well, strange that Sunday morning when he rode away."

"*Strange?*" Lige's ox eyes looked more pronounced than ever.

Gideon licked suddenly dry lips. "He said he wouldn't be in San Scipio to hear me preach, but he wouldn't say why or where he was going."

Lige's heavy fist crashed to the table, and his face mottled with anger. "Why didn't you tell me this before?"

Gideon forced himself to keep his voice low, his gaze steady. "I hoped that whatever bothered him would disappear and he'd come back."

"Is that all you know?" His father's penetrating glance backed his younger son to the wall.

"Yes." Gideon would say no more; what he suspected might or might not be true. He wouldn't distress his father more by passing on suspicion. In all probability, it would only make Lige rail against him in his blind unwillingness to admit Cyrus capable of anything less than perfection.

Gideon's second sermon went more according to what he had prepared. After fasting and prayer, he was able to lay aside the fact of Cyrus's continued absence and concentrate.

At dawn on Monday morning, Lige rose and announced he would ride to El Paso. "Will you come with me?" he asked Gideon.

Used to being ordered and not invited, Gideon hid his astonishment and agreed. During the long ride, the intangible silence between them reminded Gideon of those eerie moments in the sage before the storm. They found the rancher who had horses to sell, and Lige discreetly led the conversation around to what buyers had been there. "One of the men from San Scipio appeared mighty interested," he said. "A little taller than my son here. Heavier, but similar coloring."

The rancher shook his head. "No one like that's been around here. I'd shore have remembered." He brightened. "Long as you're here, d'yu see anything yu like?"

Before Lige could say no, a high-stepping sorrel caught Gideon's attention. "I'd like to look at the mare," he told the rancher.

A close inspection and short ride resulted in the purchase of Dainty Bess, who had won Gideon's heart with her frisky but gentle ways.

"Yu're a good judge of horse flesh," the former owner admitted. "I'da took her back with me 'cept it's too far."

52

Gideon transferred saddle and bridle, attached a lead line for the horse he had ridden to El Paso, and swung aboard his new mount. "Thanks," he called. When they crossed the first hill and left the ranch behind them, he commented, "Mother will enjoy riding this horse — that is, when I'm not on her!"

"How can you be so all-fired excited over buying a horse when your brother's off God-knows-where?" Lige's criticism effectively doused Gideon's attempts at conversation. Even though he knew his father spoke from the depths of misery and concern, Gideon's old resentment returned in full force.

As much as I can and as often as my duties to the church allow, I'll try to take Cyrus's place, he vowed. He knew it wouldn't be easy. Five years had taken a toll on the range skills he once had. Sometimes he took longer doing chores or his hands proved awkward in roping. Most often Lige said nothing, yet Gideon felt the same second-best feeling he'd experienced through the years. Even if he could ride and rope and brand full-time, he'd never be Cyrus. For that, Lige couldn't forgive him.

He often felt as if the weeks following Cyrus's departure were a stack of dynamite just waiting for a spark to set it off. Once it blew, life would never be the same. To make things worse, Gideon ran into a problem with his ministry. In his naivete, he had thought all God would require of him would be to preach, visit, and comfort. He soon discovered the folly of his thinking. Time after time, he called on God to give him strength and patience with his congregation. Good folk they were, but all too human. Gideon wished he had a peso for every time he had to become a peacemaker; a sermon was sorely needed on the subject of putting aside petty differences and pride and jealousy so the Word of God could be proclaimed.

Naomi Scott proved to be a valuable ally when it came to socializing. "Just don't pay any more attention to one family than another," she quietly advised. "If you call on the Simpsons, then make sure that within a few days you also call on the Blacks, McKenzies, and Porters. Things will settle down in time, but for now everyone wants to make sure they get equal attention from the new minister." Her smile died. "And, Gideon, beware of Lucinda Curtis." Real anxiety puckered her brow. "She's spoiled and bent on getting her own way. More than one cowboy has had to leave town because of her wild tales, which," she added, "I just don't believe. Lucinda isn't that pretty, even with all her specially bought clothes and haughty ways."

Gideon sighed and ran his fingers through his now sun-streaked hair. "Why didn't they warn us in school how silly young women can be?" He laughed ruefully. "I can't physically drink gallons of lemonade or spare the time to spend afternoons in cool courtyards! Yet every unmarried female in San Scipio seems to feel such activities are part of my job. Most of them are nice enough, but sometimes I feel the way a jackrabbit must feel when being chased. As for Lucinda," he said grimacing, "she must have taken a course in tracking her prey. How she knows where I'm going to be and manages to arrive just when I'm leaving is beyond me." He thought of the tall, thin girl with the straw-colored hair and faded gray eyes that could melt with admiration or flash pure steel when crossed. "What can I do about it?"

Naomi thought for a long time, her hands strangely idle, her blue eyes deep and considering. "Perhaps you can do nothing except to be very careful. Time will take care of the problem." A dimple danced in one cheek, and her eyes sparkled. "One of these days, the Lord will send a special person into your life. Not a butterfly who knows little more than how to preen and chase, but a real woman who will love, cherish, and complete your life."

On impulse, Gideon decided to tell her about Emily Ann. "Always the Southern belle, she would have married me if I'd agreed to remain in Louisiana and take over a church. She was sure her father could arrange such a position." He laughed. "Once I saw how shallow she was inside, I dropped off her list of admirers. Wonder how many others have been on it since I left New Orleans?" He took his mother's hand. "A long time ago, I decided that until I met someone like you, I'd go it alone. Not really alone, I have my Lord. But sometime . . ." He couldn't voice the longing he felt to have a companion, one who would support and love him, bear his children, and grow old with him.

Gideon remembered that conversation, and once or twice in the next few weeks, he even hesitantly approached God about it. Although he loved his work, the natural longings for a home of his own stirred him more than at any time before. He had so much time for reflection, especially riding Dainty Bess, a sure-footed mare that needed little guidance. While he rode the range or into canyons to visit isolated ranches or for pleasure, Gideon not only came closer to God but permitted himself to dream.

Now and then he caught qualities in one San Scipio woman or another that he admired but never in Lucinda Curtis. Always courteous, he nevertheless had a hundred valid reasons for turning down the supper invitations at her home unless others would be present. The same held true for lingering after church until everyone had gone except Lucinda, who expected to be walked home. Gideon became adept at making sure a group remained to discuss music or basket dinners. He also used the distance between the Circle S and San Scipio as an excuse until it grew more threadbare than the strip of carpet in the entryway of the town's only boardinghouse.

One afternoon the young minister had just finished posting a notice on the church door about special services he planned to hold, when Lucinda appeared. Trapped by his well-bred upbringing, Gideon would only politely greet the pink-gowned maiden.

"Do let us go inside. It's more comfortable."

"Why, don't you think it's nice out here?" Gideon motioned to an inviting bench he had recently placed in a shaded area. Not for a gold mine would he enter the church building and give her an opportunity to start talk as she had done with others. "I only have a little time. What can I do for you, Miss Curtis?"

"Please call me Lucinda." She blushed and looked down, but no modesty appeared in her eyes when she looked up again. "It's so much friendlier." She held out a white, well-cared-for, and obviously useless hand.

Gideon pretended not to see it and ushered her to the bench. "What was it you wanted?" He'd be hanged if he'd call her Lucinda.

"I, we, well, some of your congregation are concerned over your having to ride in from the Circle S." She lowered her lashes in an imitation of Emily Ann when she wanted her own way. "Autumn will come soon, then winter. We'd never forgive ourselves if you lost your strength from overwork."

Thunderstruck at the idea of her interference, Gideon couldn't say a word.

"Papa agrees with me, with us."

He would, Gideon thought sourly. Tom Curtis's spineless demeanor when it came to his only child was the stuff of legend in San Scipio. The storekeeper's pride and blind adoration of his child even outranked Lige Scott's.

"Anyway, when I just up and said it shouldn't happen, Papa said he'd be glad to build a room on our house just for you." She clasped her hands together and laughed, but Gideon saw the gloating triumph she couldn't hide. "You'll be like one of the family."

It took all his Christian charity not to shake her silly shoulders until she rattled like the doll she was. Gideon stood. "I'm in perfect health, Miss Curtis. Thank you for the offer." He couldn't manage to say he appreciated it. "I wouldn't even consider such an arrangement." With the cunning he'd developed against her wiles, he said frankly, "I'm sure you're aware there is already jealousy in the congregation." He forced himself to smile. "Such a move could create problems and charges of favoritism." He lowered his voice confidentially. "A young minister living in a home where there's an unmarried woman . . ." He let his voice drift off. "You can see, it just wouldn't do." Could even Lucinda Curtis swallow that serving of applesauce?

It slid down smoothly. "Oh, Reverend, why, I never once thought of that. What must you think of me?" Crocodile tears swam in her eyes. Fortunately, she didn't give Gideon a chance to reply. "We'll forget the whole thing, shall we?" She rose. "I really mustn't keep you." She gave him an arch smile. "It is so nice when a young man considers a woman's reputation."

For one moment, Gideon thought he would ruin the whole thing by laughing in her face. Instead, he told her, "A woman just can't be too careful."

Lucinda glanced at him sharply, and he wondered if she were remembering the rumors she had started about those cowboys. "Thank you, Reverend. Do you have time to walk me home?"

Not by a long shot, he wanted to tell her. Instead, he said, "No, but thanks again for your, er, concern." She picked her way across the churchyard, then stopped to wave gaily before she turned the corner. Not until he mounted Dainty Bess and got a mile out of town did he vent his anger and disgust by urging the faithful horse into a dead run.

CHAPTER 4

Judith Butler adjusted the mosquito netting over four-year-old Joel's small bed and swallowed hard. The small blond replica of Millicent lay in a spread-eagle position as usual. Flushed with sleep, his cheeks rosy and curly hair tangled, he tugged at Judith's heartstrings. Terror rose within her. What if she should lose him after all her struggles in the past four years to fulfill the promise she had given her dying half sister?

Judith's knees weakened, and she dropped into a shabby chair next to the sleeping boy. She rested her tired head crowned with its coronet of dark brown braids against a pale, slender hand whose calloused palm told her story of hardship. The dark brown eyes that lit with twin candles when she smiled closed. *Dear God, what am I going to do?* she silently prayed.

Only this morning her landlady had reluctantly told her she couldn't keep Joel and her much longer unless they paid something. The worn woman looked away as if ashamed to see the fear Judith knew sprang to her face.

Judith coughed as she explained, "Just as soon as I'm a little stronger, I'll be able to get work. I appreciate all you've done for us, caring for Joel when I had the fever. Please don't send us away."

The landlady's eyes filled with tears. "My dear, if I had money to buy food, I would never let you go. But with my man helpless ever since the carriage accident, I have to think of him, too. Don't you have something else you can sell?"

Judith thought of the few remaining pieces of jewelry that had brought in but a pittance when the larger pieces had been sold. The barren room she and Joel shared in the ruins of an old New Orleans house had been stripped one by one of the fine, mahogany pieces that once stood in the Butler home. Now only two cheap beds, a cracked bowl and pitcher, and little else remained. Precious Joel had made a game out of seeing their furniture go.

"It's like living in a tepee," he said with his enchanting grin, which showed small even teeth and set his blue eyes sparkling. " 'Sides, we've got you and me."

Judith's slender shoulders convulsed in a shudder. Her long illness had put a sudden end to the needlework that had supplied enough extra money to pay for their room and simple meals. Even now her hands shook so that she couldn't hold the needle. Unwilling to disturb Joel's slumbers with her agitation, Judith quietly rose and crossed the almost-empty room to kneel beside the limp curtain that sifted daylight from the single window. She unfastened the window and swung it open, hoping for a little relief from the early summer heat. A few weeks from now, it would be unbearable. Even if she could afford to stay, how could she and Joel live through another summer in this furnace of an attic? She longingly thought of her parents, both casualties of the war: her father in battle, her mother from worry and illness. The little room faded, replaced by her own merry cry and pattering feet down the steps of the beautiful home that had once been hers. . . .

"Father's come! Millie, he's here." Six-year-old Judith ran to greet him, closely followed by nine-year-old Millicent who, in spite of being older, clung to the more daring Judith and leaned on her for strength. As fair as Judith was dark, she had adored her half sister from the time their father laid the baby carefully in her arms. "A present for you, Millicent, my dear. Your own baby sister."

"I'll need my good older daughter to help me care for her," the second Mrs. Butler, who had never seemed anything but a real mother to Millie, added. She had married Mr. Butler a little over a year after his first wife died, so Millicent never knew any other mother.

Now she laughed and sped after Judith but stopped short on the wide veranda. "Why, Father, you're a *soldier!*"

"Isn't he beautiful?" Judith scampered around the tall, gray-clad man whose grim face relaxed into a smile when he caught her up in his arms. He held out his hand to Millicent.

"You're going to fight the nasty Yankees, aren't you?" Judith slid to the ground and leaned companionably against him with Millicent on his other side.

"Child, just because others don't believe as we do doesn't make them nasty," he protested. Deep lines etched his face. "I pray to God I never have to take a life. God created Northerners and Southerners alike, and He doesn't love us any more than He loves those who see things differently."

His wife joined them, fear and trouble in

her pretty face, the features Judith had inherited distorted with care. "If only God would stop this awful happening." Tears sprang to her large brown eyes, but she impatiently dashed them away.

"Girls, I don't know how long I am going to be gone," Gerald Butler said somberly. "I wish I didn't have to go at all, but I must. Always remember this: No matter how far away I am, every night just before the sun goes down and every morning when it rises, I'll be thinking of you and praying for you. Be good soldiers. Take care of your precious mama and each other."

Childish joy in his appearance fled. Judith and Millicent clasped his hands. Their mother took their other hands, and the prayer that followed burned into the children's minds, along with the special look he gave their mother before he mounted and rode off to war, his shoulders proud and square.

For a time their world of gracious living and love continued in much the same way. When the long lists of casualties began arriving, all traces of gentility faded. Gerald Butler's prayer was granted. He fell in his first battle without ever having fired a shot, his commanding officer wrote in a sympathetic letter. As life went ahead in its new order of living under Yankee control, Judith couldn't even remember when things were different. But when at last the fighting ended and troops withdrew, as great a horror as the occupation by Northern forces confronted the Butlers.

Even her great love for her daughter and stepdaughter couldn't rally Mrs. Butler enough to overcome the loss of the only man she had ever loved. Although she held on through the war, shortly afterward, she fell ill with swamp fever. A few weeks later, she died, leaving a bewildered ten- and thirteen-year-old to face life with only God as their protector. Distant relatives offered to take the girls but not together. Older than their actual years because of the tragedies they had faced, Millicent and Judith clung more closely than ever. They unearthed the family treasures their mother had managed to secrete and keep hidden for all the long years and sought lodging with an old friend who welcomed them.

Life's cruel blows continued. When the family friend died, the girls moved on from place to place. Millicent grew thin and pale from kitchen work once done by Negro slaves. Judith sewed long hours until her small fingers sometimes bled from the coarse materials. Yet they could not and would not be separated.

Days and weeks limped into years. At seventeen and fourteen, their contrasting beauty attracted attention. Yet the modest upbringing and Christian principles instilled in them so long ago kept them aloof from the gaiety with which some tried to forget the past. Sometimes they shyly talked of the future.

"How will I know when I'm in love?" Judith demanded and bit off the thread from the seam she had just finished. Her plain dark garb worn from necessity and not choice added little to her beauty, but her fresh face and sparkling eyes needed no enhancement.

Millicent's fair face shone flower-pale against her drab clothing. "I always think that if someday someone looks at me the way Father looked at Mama just before he rode away, I'll know he loves me."

"I remember that!" Judith dropped her sewing. "I don't remember, though. Did Mama look the same way?"

"Yes." A smile curved Millicent's lips upward in the gentle way that made her resemble the Madonna Judith had seen in a painting. Her eyes held dreams and softness. "Dear Judith, how blessed we are to have such memories. God has indeed been good to us all these years." She trembled, and her smile faded. "When I think how we could have been taken away from each other, it frightens me." Her blue eyes grew feverish, and she clutched her arms together across her thin body. "I think I'd rather die than to have that ever happen."

"Silly, no one's going to separate us." Judith deliberately soothed her sister, as she had done since childhood, when she realized her own strength and Millicent's frailty. "Oh, I suppose if we get married, we might not live together, but let's marry gentlemen who will let us stay close."

Twin red spots burned in Millicent's cheeks and provided unusual color. "I'd like to see any man even *try* to separate me from my sister!"

Judith's mouth dropped open. Seldom did Millie exert herself, but she certainly sounded positive now. "Why don't we wait and worry about it when it happens?" she suggested practically. "In the meantime, there's enough light for me to whip in another seam." She bent to her work, but soon the flying needle slowed and stopped. "My idea of heaven is to never, ever have to sew another garment."

"Judith!" Millicent gasped. "Don't be sacrilegious."

She looked up in honest surprise. "God says we're supposed to ask for what we want, and I'm asking that He let me do something else when I get to heaven besides sew." She giggled, and even pious Millie couldn't resist her mirth. "Maybe all the robes of righteousness will be already made by the time I get there."

"My stars, you have funny ideas." Her sister stared at her and shook her head. "When I think of heaven, I think of God and Jesus and Father and Mother and my own mother."

"I do, too," Judith said in a small voice. "I just wish Jesus would come back soon." She threw down her sewing, and tears that had been bottled up for months fell. "Oh, Millie, will we ever really be happy again?"

The older girl knelt beside her and put both arms around her. "Life is hard, but God takes care of us, and we can be happy knowing our family is with Him. Think of all the soldiers and families who don't know Jesus, how much harder it is for them." She comforted Judith, and their mingled tears helped to wash away sad memories.

The summer of 1869 proved to be both disturbing and joyous. Judith learned that Millicent had met a dashing young gentleman who admired her and sought her out at every opportunity. *If Millie is in love, why doesn't she bring the young man to meet me?* she wondered.

"I will," Millicent promised, but she sent a sad glance around their poorly furnished abode. "It's just that we've no place, and —"

"If it's good enough for us, it should be good enough for any gentleman caller," Judith interrupted fiercely.

"Don't you see? We can't *have* gentlemen callers here without a chaperone." Millicent smiled in a way that made her sister lonely for the first time. Hot jealousy against this stranger who had come between them joined forces with the protective instinct she had always displayed toward Millie.

"It's all right, really it is," Millicent assured her. "He's tallish and as blond as I am. When he looks at me, I —" She broke off, unable to express what she felt.

"Do you feel the way Father and Mama did that day?" Judith whispered.

The ecstasy in Millie's face stilled her sister's protests. "Oh, yes. If he doesn't love me, I don't know how I can go on." A dark shadow crossed her sweet face. "There are so many girls. They come and go at the place I work. Why should anyone so wonderful even look at a humble serving maid?"

"Anyone that wonderful would be bound to see past your job," Judith snapped, still troubled. "Hasn't he even asked to meet me?"

"N–no. But I've told him all about you, how clever you are with a needle and how we've stayed together all this time." Doubt crept into the blue eyes. "He just laughs and says there's plenty of time. Since I'm only seventeen and don't have a guardian, I suppose he wants to make sure I know what I want."

Judith's lips formed the question, but she couldn't quite ask, *Do you? Do you, Millie?* Instead, she held her tongue and prayed that God would care for her sister and keep her safely.

A few weeks later, Judith received the shock of her life. She came home dog-weary from hunting new quarters that might be more pleasant than those they now had. Never had she seen Millie more radiant. *"Look!"* Her sister held out her slender hand. A shiny gold ring encircled her finger.

"Millicent, you haven't, you didn't . . . *Where did you get that ring?"* Judith stared in horror, her stomach churning.

"It's my wedding ring." Happiness and regret blended in her voice. "I'm so sorry I couldn't tell you, but we, I knew how opposed you'd be to my marrying so young and especially when you haven't even met him, and —"

Judith cut through her babble. "You actually got married without ever telling me?" Suspicion crystallized. "Was this *his* idea?"

"Please don't feel badly, Dear." Even Millicent's contrite apology couldn't dim the shining radiance of her face. "Everything is going to be wonderful. I'll just be gone a few days for a short honeymoon, then we'll have a home together for always. My new husband says he will be glad to have you live with us." The sound of carriage wheels outside the window sent her scurrying to look out. She snatched a valise from the bed. "Come meet him before we go."

Judith hesitated, feeling caught in a moment somewhere between the order that had been their lives and the uncertainty ahead. "I'd rather wait until you come back," she managed.

"I understand." The sweet smile that characterized Millicent showed that she did, but her new allegiance overcame even the bonds of sisterhood. With a warm squeeze of Judith's shoulders, she sped toward the door. Her heels clattered on the staircase, and the lower door banged shut.

"What am I doing?" Judith frantically

came out of the shocked trance into which she'd fallen. She raced to the window and leaned out. *"Wait!"* The word couldn't compete with the street noises and laughter of children. Millicent's face turned upward, but Judith knew she didn't look toward the window but into her new husband's face.

I must see what he looks like, she thought quickly. Judith leaned out farther but only glimpsed blond hair and the back of the man's head as he helped Millicent into the carriage.

"Wait!" she called again. "Millicent, I'll be right down!" Even as she called, she knew it was too late. The carriage wheels began to turn, and the harness jingled as her sister rode into a new life, leaving Judith behind.

It's only for a few days, she told herself again and again. She made excuses for Millie's absence, saying she had gone away with friends, yet for three nights Judith cried herself to sleep. There had to be something wrong with a man who would not only hastily marry a seventeen-year-old but who did it furtively and without her only close relative's knowledge. He must have known how Judith would object; perhaps he was afraid she would sway her sister against such an act. In the silence of the evenings, Judith often heard thunder in the distance that warned of a storm waiting to break. Was this small island of silence during Millicent's honeymoon also the prelude to a storm, one that would shatter Judith's world and perhaps Millie's as well?

All through those long, waiting hours beat the question, *What shall I do if she never comes back? I don't even know her husband's name!* Judith sought her Lord as never before in her young life. She stormed the very gates of heaven on Millicent's behalf and her own. She prayed for forgiveness for the hatred in her heart toward the man who had stolen Millie's love. Sometimes she even cried out for God to take her away from an uncaring world that had hurt her so deeply.

Too upset and ill to work, Judith lay on her bed listening for the sound of carriage wheels. A dozen times she leaped up and pelted to the window. When the right carriage finally came and stopped, she had fallen into a fitful sleep, her tear-stained face in the curve of one arm. Millicent found her that way, and compassion filled her. She slipped back downstairs as arranged, but with the word Judith should not be disturbed. "You can meet her tomorrow," she told her husband. "I'll stay with her tonight."

He quickly agreed, and Millie's heart

swelled with love and pride in his understanding. She watched the carriage roll out
of sight, thrilling that such a man had ever
desired her. Then she went back to her
sister, her heart filled with happy plans for
the future.

"Millie?" Judith roused when Millicent
reentered their room. "Is it really you? I
dreamed you went off and didn't come
back. I felt so alone. I didn't know what to
do or where to go." She broke off. "Where
is he?"

Millicent hugged her and laughed and
removed a charming new hat. "We decided
I'd stay here tonight. Tomorrow —" She
lowered her voice to a mysterious tone.
"Tomorrow we're going to see about finding a proper house. Oh, Judith, I've never
been so happy in my whole life!"

Judith had never been more miserable. Yet
curiosity pushed aside foreboding. "Where
did you go?"

"To a wonderful inn just north of town.
Then we shopped, and see?" She whirled,
and her light blue summer dress flounced
around her. "That's not all." She tore open
a large parcel she had carried in with her.
"Your favorite colors." A fluffy yellow and
white dress tumbled out. "We found a shop
where they sold dresses already made. It

should fit. I just remembered that you're four inches taller." Millicent held the dress up to her petite five-foot, four-inch frame where it dragged on the floor.

Her troubles momentarily forgotten, Judith tried on the dress. It settled over her young body as if it had been designed exclusively to highlight her dark brown hair and eyes. "It's lovely, the prettiest dress I've had since —"

"I know." Millicent's shine dimmed. "But how glad Father and Mama would be to know we're going to be happy again." She laughed and confessed, "Don't ever tell anyone, but even on my honeymoon, I missed you so much I could hardly wait to get back to tell you how wonderful life is going to be. After tomorrow, we'll never have to worry about a place to live or having enough money to pay our way." Her sapphire eyes sparkled. "We'll wear our new dresses."

Somehow the excited girls managed to sleep a little. Judith found herself so caught up in anticipation that the little worries that pricked her heart like dressmakers' pins lost themselves. By ten o'clock, they had primped and preened until every shining hair lay in place. For the first time, Millicent wound Judith's shining braids around her head in a coronet. "The new dress needs a new hairstyle," she announced. "Besides, fourteen is no longer a child."

Judith found herself blushing up to the high lacy collar of the pretty gown. Could that really be her own image in the mirror? The girl with rosy cheeks and smiling mouth? How different from the way she had felt while Millicent had been gone! "Pooh," she told her reflection. "I worry too much." She turned toward her sister, lovely in the pale blue gown and the serenity Judith knew came from happiness. She wanted to open her heart, to confess all her doubts, yet doing so would only hurt Millie. Perhaps someday when they were both old women, they would laugh together over the younger sister's misgivings. Now they were too silly, too unreal in the clear sunny morning to utter. Not one bitter drip should be allowed to spoil Millicent's perfect day, Judith vowed with all the passion of her years. *She may never again be exactly this eager and happy.*

The thought startled her. Why shouldn't Millicent have hundreds of happy, eager days? How perfectly ridiculous to allow her own trepidation to color her judgment and imagine all kinds of ridiculous impossibilities. She twitched her skirt again and strained for the sound of carriage wheels.

They did not come.

The clock that had been in the Butler family for generations slowly ticked off the seconds, the minutes, the hours. At first Millicent laughed and admitted what a sleepyhead her husband had proven to be. He liked to stay up late and rise at his leisure. The clock ticked on, relentlessly passing noon, one o'clock, two. By three, Judith had lost interest in her pretty dress and changed. "You don't think there's been an accident," she finally said, then wished she'd kept silent.

Millicent's face turned the shade of parchment. "Surely he would have managed to send me word." She slowly rose. "We must go to where he lodges immediately."

"Wait, Millie. A carriage just stopped."

Color flowed back into her sister's face. "Thank God!" She ran to the door and flung it open. "My dear, where have you been?"

CHAPTER 5

Judith followed her sister to the door and glanced first at the Negro, then at Millicent, whose hand went to her throat. "Who are you, and what do you want?" she demanded.

"I have a message for the other young lady," The man held out a folded paper, turned on his heel, and hurried down the stairs.

Judith glared at his retreating back but turned back to her sister when she heard a low moan. "Millie, what is it? Is your husband hurt? Do we need to go to him?"

Millicent tottered back inside the open door and sank to a shabby settee. Every trace of color had drained from her face. She wordlessly held out the paper, and Judith grabbed it from her.

My dear,
    New Orleans just isn't the place for me, I'm leaving for home today. I have

79

wronged you by going through with the marriage ceremony. Forgive me, if you can.

There was no signature.

Judith crumpled the page the way she wished she could crumple the man responsible for the devastation of her beloved sister. "How could anyone be so cruel?" Fury threatened to choke her.

"I thought he loved me." Millicent looked as if she had been stabbed.

"Quick, what is his address?" Judith sprang to the occasion. "Surely he can't have gone yet!"

The pride of her father stiffened Millie's spine. Her blue eyes flashed. "Do you think I want him to come back after this? Never!" New dignity raised her head and dried her tears.

"You don't love him any longer?" Judith's brain spun.

"Loving someone has little to do with honor and respect," Millicent quietly said as her fingers mercilessly wrung a handkerchief. "Even if he came back, this would always be between us." A little color returned to her face. "It isn't even a matter of forgiving, which I could do. I'd have to, according to the Bible. But forcing him to stay when he wants to be elsewhere . . ." Her voice trailed into silence, the same silence that had hovered in the poorly furnished room while she had been away and Judith waited.

"What will we do now?" Judith asked. For the first time in her life, she felt incapable of making decisions.

Millie's lips set in a straight line. "No one knows of our marriage except we three. The family I work for granted me the time off for a rest. Tomorrow I will go back." Never had she appeared stronger. "We will go on as we have." She looked around the room and shuddered with distaste. "As soon as we're able, we will move to another part of the city and leave no address."

"But what if he should come back?" Judith cried, her heart aching at the stony look in Millicent's eyes.

"Dear sister, if he really wants to find me, he will." Long lashes swept down to hide Millie's eyes and made little dark half moons on her white cheeks. "I don't think he will, though." Her lips trembled, and she hastened to the window and looked out as if seeing far beyond the familiar street below.

Through a relentless summer and a welcome fall, there was no sign of the peripatetic bridegroom. Millicent and Judith sold a few more heirlooms and established themselves in new quarters. One autumn day, when leaves whirled before the wind, Millie told her sister she had an announcement to make. She stood by the window as she so often did.

In the silence, Judith's heart pounded for no apparent reason. What could make Millie look like that, exalted, yet despairing.

"I am with child."

At first Judith could but stare. A multitude of feelings rushed over her: shock, disbelief, even admiration that her sister could be so calm.

"You're going to have to help me," Millicent went on. "The baby will be born next spring, late April or early May. Between now and then, we must save every penny we can. No matter how hard it is, I'll never give my baby away for others to raise."

Judith ran to her and hugged her fiercely. "Of course you won't! We'll take care of the baby and —" She broke off. "Millie, don't you think you should let him know? You could send a letter to where he used to live. . . ."

Millie looked full into her sister's eyes. "No, I thought it all out before I told you. This is my child. He forfeited the right to it by leaving, even though he had no way of knowing there would be a baby." Her eyes glowed with feverish intensity. "Don't you see? He comes from a well-to-do family. Suppose he claimed the child? We have no money to fight for my baby." She caught Judith's hand and held it until the younger girl winced. "Promise that no matter what happens, you won't let him take the baby."

A warning flutter inside Judith died before her sister's agony. Making such a promise might be wrong, but Millicent's peace of mind had to be assured. "I promise." She squeezed the clutching hand. Yet another clutching hand, cold and frightening, held her heart in a grip so powerful, she wanted to cry out.

The coming of the child changed everything. They first needed to find a place where neither was known or Millicent's condition would bring shame and speculation. After much searching, they finally relocated in a drab but still respectable boardinghouse. Millie disguised herself with loose clothing and continued her maid's work. Judith sewed until her eyes burned. Babies needed things the sisters could ill afford, but little by little, a pitiful array of tiny garments lay waiting and ready. On the last day of April 1870, a frightened but determined Judith helped Millie in what fortunately was an easy birth and delivered a squalling but perfectly formed boy.

"We have no money for doctors," Millicent had insisted. "Babies come, and we can manage." All Judith's protests failed to sway her. "I'll be all right, and you're strong, almost fifteen years old."

The first weeks after her son's birth, Millicent's magnificent determination alone kept her going. She named the baby Joel Butler, and the little horde of money the girls had been able to save carried them through. A few times, Judith mentioned contacting the baby's father but found Millicent even more opposed than before. A few months later, a complete reversal occurred. For several days, Judith had been aware of the way Millie's gaze followed her whenever she was in the room. One fall evening, she quietly said, "I'm not sure if God will allow me to stay long enough to raise Joel." Her eyes held sadness but no fear. Judith noticed how frail she looked before she went on.

"All those months ago, I made you promise; now I want you to change your promise." The appeal in the thin face would have melted a heart carved from ice. "I still want you to keep my baby, Judith. But if the time ever comes that you are no longer able to do so, I release you from the promise not to contact Joel's father. There are papers hidden beneath the lining of the old trunk: the marriage lines, names, and addresses." She reached out and clung to Judith's hand. "Never read them or use the information unless you feel you have no choice but to lose Joel."

"I promise." Judith's throat felt thick. She tried to cover it by saying, "Here we are at dusk, talking gloomy thoughts!" She lit a candle, and its flickering light steadied into a glow that dispelled some of the shadows. "There, is that better?"

Millicent roused herself from her private thoughts, and they said no more. Yet the knowledge of the pact between them made Judith feel old beyond her years. Her gaze strayed toward the box they had carefully lined with soft material for a crib. He was so good, like a little golden-haired angel. He seldom cried, and his large, intelligent eyes and well-shaped head made him seem older than his few months on earth.

"Dear God," Judith whispered long after her sister slept that night. "Please, don't take Millicent. You and she and Joel are all I have left." Waves of loneliness washed through her. A few minutes later, the peace of her heavenly Father descended, and the troubled young woman slept.

As if relieved to have talked things out, Millicent rallied. She continued to work, while Judith sewed at home and cared for Joel. November and December passed. During an unusually chilly January, Millicent contracted a bad cold that kept her home. She arranged with her employer to send Judith in her place. The hardest thing was not allowing Joel to come near her lest he also become ill. By February, Millie still could not work, and a cough lingered that frightened Judith, no matter how much her sister tried to assure her. She called a doctor, who silently examined Millicent and shook his head. Judith followed him into the hall.

"I can't do anything. She let it go too long." His keen eyes bored into Judith. "You'd better contact some relatives and make arrangements for yourself and the little boy."

Somehow Judith managed to murmur her thanks and pay him as well, her heart filled with terror. If he took it on himself to let the authorities know if Millicent died, they would come and get Joel.

Millie brought it up when Judith went back into their room. Thin and wasted, she ordered her sister to get everything packed.

"You don't have to tell me what the doctor said," she began. "I think I've always known how things would be. Don't cry, Judith. There isn't time. I want you to take the last of Mama's jewelry and sell it now. Sew the money into the bodice of your dress." She took a deep breath and coughed until exhausted, but her spirit permitted no giving up. "The hardest thing you've ever done is what you must do soon. As soon as God takes me to be with Father and Mama, you must flee. Don't wait for anyone to come. When the landlady doesn't hear stirring, she will come up and find me."

"That's horrible!" Judith cried. "I can't do it!"

Millicent rose up on one elbow. "You must. If you love me, grant my last wish. What does it matter who buries me or where?" Fever painted red flags in the sunken white cheeks. "Don't you see? Joel will be taken from you if you don't escape with him." She panted, more beautiful in her illness than ever before. "Now go and sell the jewelry. I've remembered the name of an old friend who may take you in and never tell anyone. It's written down in the front of the big Bible." She fell back to the thin pillow, her eyes filled with pity.

"Poor Judith. So young to have all this

tragedy. Please don't mourn for me. I'll be with loved ones, and soon you and my little son will come. Even if it isn't for years, it will seem in the twinkling of an eye for me." She coughed again. "Dear little sister, God will give you strength to do what you are required. He will uphold and sustain you. Now, go."

Unable to argue in the face of such courage, Judith got out the last of the jewels, donned a cloak, and hurried to the man who had purchased other items from them. Back with the money, she discovered that Millie had been doing more planning.

"Go right away and see if Mama's friend will take us, but don't say when we're coming," she ordered. "Then tell our landlady that I'm sick and we'll be moving soon. Get a drayman to come for what furniture we have left."

Again the necessity of providing for the future lent strength to the failing young woman. For several days, she kept on in spite of her obvious weakness. Not until every direction had been carried out and only a pallet on her floor remained did Millicent relax.

"It won't be long," she told Judith. "But I am so happy you will keep Joel. Remember your promise." She fell asleep with a smile on her pale lips.

All night Judith kept vigil. The light of a guttering candle showed when Millicent's earthly sleep changed. Not one tear fell. Judith had gone beyond that in the hours and days before her sister's death. She had to be strong for Joel.

After a final survey of the room, Judith left the bit of money she could scarcely afford to repay the landlady for her trouble in contacting the authorities. On a scrap of paper, she wrote, *I'm sorry it isn't more, but I must care for the child.* Once again she was glad that the room had been listed under "M. Greene," Millie's middle name. In the first rays of morning, she quietly took the sleeping child from his nest at the foot of Millicent's pallet and slipped into the mists of dawn.

Judith would never clearly remember how she and Joel existed. She stretched the bit of money in her dress while making her small charge's clothing from the leftover pieces of her sewing jobs. One by one, the familiar childhood furniture pieces vanished. Yet Joel thrived and provided joy to the girl's sad heart. While others her age danced and frolicked, she held her head high and cared for Joel. Still a child at heart in many ways, she played with him and made up games. When time permitted, she took him for walks, and although many times she ached to buy him all the things others had, he never asked for anything.

Once in awhile the old friend who now served as her landlady cared for the charming little boy while Judith delivered her work. She didn't care to allow her personal situation and business world to touch by taking him with her.

Weeks, then months, then years passed. Soon Joel would have his fourth birthday; Judith, her nineteenth. She had developed into a tall, slender young woman whose dark brown eyes still lit with twin candles when she played with Joel. Her shining coronet of dark brown braids suited her as no other hairstyle. Even Joel, who liked to brush her hair at night, thought it prettiest when coiled around her shapely head.

Because of Millicent's experience with a faithless lover, Judith almost innately distrusted men. Those she met through business who showed open admiration received instant rebuffs. Millie had been so sure of her happiness, perhaps too sure. Yet Judith could never fully regret the sad circumstances when Joel confidingly tucked his hand in hers and said he loved her.

If only she hadn't allowed herself to grow

rundown by skimping on meals so she could put away extra for Joel! Suddenly Judith's secure world crashed. Sickness struck and lingered. Panicky, she tried to continue her work and could not. Even when the fever left, she crept through the days like a ghost of her former strong self. During her delirious periods, the thought hammered until she thought she would go mad. *The promise. The promise. I must keep my promise to Millicent.* Part of the time she couldn't remember what it was, and she felt too sick to care. She fought with all her remaining strength and came back from the brink of death. If anything happened to her, no one would know who Joel was! Could it be right for him to be put away and cheated out of his rightful inheritance? Over and over she considered the circumstances. If only God would help her know what to do now that she simply could not care for herself and Joel as she had done these long, hard years. . . .

Joel moved in his sleep, and Judith returned from her long mental journey to the past. She reached beneath the netting and straightened his tangle of sheets, smothering the noble brow. A wave of love stronger than any she had experienced flowed through her. She couldn't care more for Joel if he were her own son. Wasn't he her own, given to her by Millicent?

"I have to decide what to do, heavenly Father." She resumed her post at the window. "It may mean losing him, but I can't take the chance of growing ill again and not being able to provide for him." Her gaze strayed to the old trunk that held their meager supply of clothing and worldly goods. Dread filled her, yet the time had come for action. She resolutely stood and crossed to the trunk. Her hands shook so she could barely open it, but she finally lifted the lid and propped it back.

"Papers beneath the lining," she muttered. She loosened stitches so tiny as to be nearly invisible, her throat tight at the thought of Millie secreting the pages until no one would suspect the trunk contained any item but the obvious.

The few papers crackled as she withdrew them. Such a small witness to the short time Millicent had loved and rejoiced and found happiness to sustain her. Judith had to blink away the tears that persisted in coming between her and the important documents. She barely glanced at the wedding certificate. What she needed was an address, somewhere to send a letter admitting the existence of a four-year-old boy for whom she could no longer provide.

A scrawled page in the same handwriting she'd seen in the note delivered that fateful day almost five years earlier caught her attention. She snatched it up and scanned it in the fading light. "Oh, no!" She desperately pulled aside the screening curtain to get more light. Somehow moisture had seeped into the old trunk and the address was unreadable.

Judith frantically dug behind the lining for other pages but found none. She turned to the marriage lines and gave a soft cry of gladness. Clear and bright, the date of July 29, 1869, proclaimed to a more or less interested world that Millicent Butler and Gideon Carroll Scott had been united in holy matrimony.

Her gladness turned to despair. What good was a name without an address? She had no idea where this Gideon Carroll Scott lived, either while in New Orleans or when he went back to the home he mentioned in the cruel farewell note. Millicent, usually so open, had never talked about him except the times she extracted Judith's promises concerning Joel.

"Dear God, this is a mountain neither Millie nor I expected," she whispered. In spite of the warm evening, her hands felt icy and nerveless. "Now what can I do?"

Should she make inquiries in New Orleans? If so, where would she start? If she went to Millicent's employer with the story of Joel's birth, they would laugh her to scorn. Millie had been proud they had never known. Besides, opening the past might prove disastrous. What did the authorities do to young women who stole away a child, leaving no trace?

Strange that the memory of her father's words when he rode off to war came back to her now. *Every night just before the sun goes down and every morning when it rises, I'll be thinking of you and praying for you.* A passionate longing for her dead father rose within Judith. How distressed he would be to see her in such straits. Yet always he had taught that her heavenly Father loved her even more than he, although to her young heart it had hardly seemed possible.

Too weary to think longer, Judith sought out her bed. She fell asleep with a prayer for direction and guidance on her lips. Morning brought Joel to her bed in his usual whirlwind manner, and for a time she forgot their uncertain future. Yet throughout the day she found herself saying over and over in her heart and mind, *God, I am helpless. It's all up to You.*

With a round-eyed Joel beside her, Judith found the strength to delve into the depths of the old trunk. "What's this?" he asked and pointed to a slight bulge in the side. His eager fingers worked the lining loose. "Why, Judith, it's *money!*"

"It can't be," she argued, but there lay a small pouch with money in it and a paper in Millicent's fine handwriting that read, "Passage money, if ever needed." How had her sister been able to put it away from their scant income? Now if Judith only knew where to go! Or should she just give the money to their landlady and hope for the best? She rejected the idea as soon as it came. Such a temporary solution wouldn't cure their problems.

That afternoon, Judith and Joel walked through the poor neighborhood just to get away from their room. Dirty newspapers swirled in the street under horses' hooves. Perhaps she should rescue one and see if anyone needed a housekeeper, someone who would allow her to bring Joel, too. Judith managed to grab a paper slightly cleaner than the others. She idly turned the pages, pausing at one that showed a small group of men in front of a stately building. If only things had been different! She'd like Joel to go to college one day, but there seemed to be little hope unless God Himself intervened in their lives.

She started to turn the page, then stopped. A frank-faced, smiling young man stared at her from beneath the headline: WEST TEXAS MAN LEADS CLASS IN ACADEMICS. Would she ever know a young man like that? Probably not, but Joel could become one. She curiously read the words beneath the picture, wondering why anyone from West Texas would be going to school in New Orleans. The next instant, she stopped breathing, only to start again when her head spun. She closed her eyes and read the caption: Local lads found it impossible to keep up with a young ministerial student from the Wild West. Gideon Carroll Scott returns to San Scipio, Texas, for his first pastorate.

CHAPTER 6

The newspaper dropped from Judith's numb fingers. Blood rushed to her head as she bent to retrieve it. Her avid gaze sought out the featured picture. Was this man a scoundrel, an utterly heartless rake who broke Millicent's heart and left behind a world of trouble and misery? Impossible! And yet, how many Gideon Carroll Scotts could there be?

He had been in New Orleans all these years, hiding under the guise of one studying to be a minister! Appalled at the further evidence of his wickedness, a rush of fury sent determination coursing through Judith's veins, bringing strength to overcome the weakness caused by her illness. *Mr. Gideon Carroll Scott has a big surprise coming,* she thought with a small amount of satisfaction. She tore out the article, stuffed it in her reticule, and managed to steady her voice. "Come, Joel. It's time for us to go home."

He trotted obediently beside her, one chubby hand confidingly in hers. Now and then he pointed with the other at some wonder: an especially colorful rose, a dog on a leash, a strutting peacock on a shady lawn. His laugh rang, and his blue eyes shaped like those of the man in the newspaper shone in the sunshine. "Look, Judy."

"Yes, Dear." Preoccupation made her answer less interested than usual. When he questioningly looked up, she hastened to add, "Aren't they beautiful?" From the time Joel first walked, he had developed an inner sense that told him when his beloved Judy was troubled. Sometimes it took all her best efforts to hide her feelings so he could be the normal, happy child God had created him to be.

As soon as Joel fell asleep after their simple supper of bread and milk, Judith got out her writing materials. Page after scorching page, she wrote to the missing Gideon Carroll Scott and ended by saying she and Joel would be on their way west by the time he received her letter.

When the white heat of anger faded, reason took over. What if by some strange quirk of fate this wasn't the man who deserted Millie? "Oh, dear God," she whispered. "It must be. I asked You for help and found the newspaper. But I have to be sure. Please guide me." For a long time, she sat there thinking and listening to Joel's even breathing. At last she reluctantly tore the letter to bits. Time enough for recrimination later. Now she must make sure of her ground. She took a clean sheet of paper and wrote a simple message:

If you are Gideon Carroll Scott, who married Millicent Butler who died in early 1871, contact me.

J. Butler

She added her current address; she must stay until she received an answer. Checking to see that Joel still slept, Judith hurried downstairs and outside to post her letter to San Scipio, Texas. Surely someone there would know Gideon Scott. The paper had named it as his hometown.

She had no choice but to use a little of the designated passage money to stave off eviction until she heard from Texas. Yet, day after sweltering day passed and no message came. Judith forced herself to take up her needle and work, even when the fabric shook in her unsteady hands.

"Why d'you work so hard, Judy?" Concern shone in Joel's eyes as he leaned against her knee.

She roused from her fatigue and smiled. "Can you keep a secret?"

"Oooh, yes." His face lighted up. "Is it a nice one?"

"It's a bi-i-i-ig secret," she solemnly told him, unwilling to label what they must do next as nice. "Don't tell anyone."

"Not even God?" he anxiously asked. "We tell Him ever'thing."

"You dear!" She laid the almost-finished garment aside and pulled him into her lap, noting how worn her dark dress had become. For a moment, a vision of a fluffy yellow and white dress danced before her to be sternly put away, as the dress had been long ago. "God already knows, but we won't tell anyone else. We're going to leave here and go on a long, long trip."

"Like Mama went to heaven?" He snuggled closer to her. "That would be nice. We could see Mama and Jesus. Maybe even God."

Judith hastily corrected the impression she had given. "Not to heaven, Joel. To Texas."

"Is that close to heaven?"

Although the memory of one man's faithlessness colored her reply, Judith felt compelled to explain the situation to Joel as best she could. "I don't think so. Joel, we've never talked much about your father's family. That's because they live in Texas, and now we may get to see them. Would you like that?"

Joel's face looked puzzled, but he nodded his head.

"This is hard for me to say to you. Your mama named you after her family when you were born because your father left New Orleans and went back to Texas. I think it's time for you to know your real name: Joel Scott." Sensing that she had imparted too much information for him to process immediately, Judith returned to the details of their impending trip. "Can you imagine what Texas will look like? Think of all the cows and horses we'll see!" From her limited supply of Texas lore, she painted an exciting picture, wanting only to cry until every tear inside her washed away her misery and the need for this hateful trip.

In spite of the silence from San Scipio, she still clung to the forlorn hope Gideon might write. But as summer relentlessly continued, Judith knew they must go. With another autumn and winter just ahead, she didn't dare chance not being able to work. After a final sleepless night of prayer, she purchased passage and left New Orleans with Joel and the shabby trunk that contained little more than their well-worn clothes, the big Bible, and the precious wedding certificate.

Dust, heat, and coarse food threatened to choke Judith, but the fear of the unknown was more unpalatable. One of few women on the trip, she endured rough men who treated her kindly and palefaced men who eyed her and attempted conversation. The endless journey sometimes made her wonder if she and Joel had been crossing Texas all their lives. Overheard conversation told her how proud Texans were of their state, and she bitterly wondered why. She spoke little with her fellow travelers and reserved all her energy for Joel, who thrived on the attention after years of being so isolated. A few times she reluctantly relinquished him to a keen-eyed driver who invited "the little feller" to ride up on top with him. Joel returned big-eyed and chattering. Long-eared jackrabbits fascinated him. Tumbleweeds made him laugh with their antics. He sniffed sagebrush and said, "It tickles." Even in her misery, Judith couldn't help seeing how the little boy brought gladness to all around him. *God, may it ever be so* became her constant prayer.

Just when the exhausted young woman felt she couldn't go on another day, their driver, Pete, bellowed out, "San Scipio comin'!"

"Son Sip-yo comin'," Joel echoed.

Judith roused from her listlessness. Torrents of weakness washed through her, but she could not give up now. She instinctively turned to her source of comfort. "Dear God," she murmured so low no one else could hear, "help me to go on in Your strength. Mine is gone."

The horses topped a hill. Interested in spite of herself, Judith looked down at San Scipio, cupped between two rises. Could that be a town, the one long and dusty street with only a few buildings on each side? She leaned forward and glimpsed other buildings back from the so-called thoroughfare. The horses picked up their pace.

"Whoa, you ornery critters!" Pete stopped the stage before the building marked GENERAL STORE in faded letters on a weather-beaten board.

Judith's spirits crashed. In her need to find Joel's father, she never once thought it would be in a place like this or that places like this even existed. "Sir, isn't there a hotel?" Her voice trembled, even though she tried to keep it steady. Pete, who had leaped down and opened the door of the stagecoach, pushed his sombrero back on his head. Trouble loomed large on his unshaven face. "Naw, and the boardin'house ain't much, either."

"Wh–where can we go?"

Pete scratched his cheek. "The Curtises have the biggest place, but yu don't wanta go there." He peered at her, and his face reddened. "Beggin' yure pardon, Ma'am. But d'yu an' the little feller have kin here?"

Judith urged Joel off her lap as she considered her answer. "Gideon Scott is a relative of ours," she said somewhat awkwardly.

Glancing from Judith to Joel, enlightenment slowly came to the driver's face. "Well, by the powers, I shoulda . . ." He quickly swallowed, then mopped his face with a trail-dusty kerchief. "Stay right here." He helped them down and to a bench away from a small group of curious onlookers. Down the street Pete went in the clumsy way Judith had come to associate with Texans, who seemed more at home on horses than on foot. She vaguely wished the driver hadn't recognized Joel's lineage, but what did it matter? Before long, San Scipio and the hills and valleys would ring with shock concerning Joel's identity.

A few minutes later, Pete returned, followed by a towheaded lad who looked to be about fifteen perched behind a high-stepping horse pulling a light buggy.

"This here's Ben. He's rarin' to drive yu to the Circle S."

"The Circle S?" Judith raised inquiring brows.

"Lige Scott's ranch." Pete swung the trunk expertly aboard the buggy and helped his former passengers up into it. "Good luck, Miss. You, too, little feller." He lowered his voice. "Don't pay no mind if Lige raves. It's his way." His smile warmed Judith's heart, and at that moment, she felt as if she were leaving her last friend. Her grizzled guardian angel tousled Joel's curls. "Don't yu fergit yure pardner Pete."

"I won't," the little boy promised.

"Neither will I." The grateful look Judith sent him brought an even deeper red to his windburned, leathery face. "Good-bye, and God bless you."

Ben touched the horse lightly with the reins, and the buggy rolled away. Judith didn't look back, but Joel turned around and waved to their benefactor.

"I'll just drive past the new church," Ben told his passengers. His eyes gleamed at the thought of driving this pale but pretty visitor and little boy all the way out to the

Circle S. The coins Pete had given him jingled merrily in his pocket. "We got ourselves the greatest preacher there ever was."

"Oh?" Judith grasped the opportunity to learn something about Gideon.

One word of polite interest was enough to loosen Ben's wagging tongue. A straw-colored lock of hair dangled on his forehead, but it didn't slow his praise. "Gideon went to N'Orleans and studied so he could be the best preacher ever. Don't see why he needed to go, but he did. Anyway, he, oh, here's the church." Ben pulled in their horse. "Door's closed. Preacher don't stick around much; too busy out visiting folks. Here, let me help you down. You can see inside, anyway."

Judith bit back tears when she observed the faithfully cared-for flowers and the obvious love that had gone into the building. Black anger for the perfidy of the minister warred with the hatred she felt for having to expose his sin and shatter the tranquil silence that surrounded the building. Inside, the presence of God hung in the quiet air. Ben nearly burst with pride, showing the careful work put into the San Scipio church.

"We all helped," he said simply. "Sometimes when I hear Gideon preach, it makes me wonder if a feller oughtn't to get right down on his knees and thank the Almighty for bringing Gideon back when he coulda had a big city church."

Judith bit her tongue to keep from shrieking out the truth. The fall of his idol might change boyish devotion to God into bitterness. *What an awful thing Gideon has done, not just to Millicent or his congregation but to himself,* she thought. Her fingers pressed the reticule that held the creased picture of him. How like an angel he looked, how like Joel. Yet hadn't Lucifer been the fairest of all before he turned from God?

Back in the buggy, Joel fell asleep in spite of the changing country through which they passed. Ben rambled on, repeating almost verbatim Gideon's first sermon and the story of his conversation. "Pushed his notes away, he did. Just stood there and talked kinda quietlike, but you coulda heard an owl hoot a mile away, everyone was so still."

Again Judith had the feeling of wrongness. Doubt assailed her. If she had spent the last of her substance to come to San Scipio and it turned out the young minister had nothing to do with Millicent and Joel, what then?

I can always sew, she told herself, but misgivings continued to attack. Not many women in this part of the country would be in need of a dressmaker or seamstress, no matter how skilled. Perhaps that family Pete had mentioned could use her services.

She took advantage of the next time Ben stopped talking to catch his breath. "Do you know the Curtis family?"

"Huh, who doesn't? Old man Curtis is the storekeeper, 'cept his high-toned wife and daughter run him and the store, too." Ben put on a falsetto voice. " 'Oh, Mr. Curtis, you mustn't even *think* of puttin' the nicest goods out for sale! Luanda's in des'prit need of a new gown for the ball.' "

"*Ball!* You have balls in San Scipio?" Judith forgot her troubles for a moment.

"Huh-uh." Ben grinned a comradely smile. "That's just what Mrs. Curtis called the big re-cep-tion she aimed to give for Gideon." The grin stretched into a guffaw. "Not on your tintype did it come off. Preacher up and said he'd rather just have folks come to church on Sundays, and he'd shake their hands after services."

"What did Mrs. Curtis say?"

"Not much, but Lucinda simpered around and told everyone how noble Gideon was until San Scipio wished she'd keep still."

Judith tried to fit what Ben related to the image of a young man so selfish he would marry a girl and walk out on her. It seemed impossible. Yet hadn't there been belated recognition in Pete's eyes when he glanced at Joel? Too weary to figure it out, she sighed until Ben stopped the winded horse on top of the mesa above the Circle S in the same place Lige and Gideon had rested weeks before.

"The Circle S," Ben said unnecessarily.

Restful. The word came to mind with Judith's first glance below. After the shock of San Scipio, she had feared a shack. Instead, she saw the red-tiled roof and cream adobe walls turned pure gold by the slanting sun. A feeling of coming home tore at Judith. Distant hills gave way to higher mountains. An eagle, twin to the one that winged in the sky to welcome Gideon home, cast its dark shadow over the trail ahead.

"It's so still." Judith automatically lowered her voice.

"Cyrus must not be home, or it wouldn't be."

Something in Ben's guarded voice made her inquire, "Who's Cyrus?"

"Gideon's brother, but they ain't alike." Ben miraculously stopped talking and urged the horse forward down the steep decline to the valley floor. "Circle S's the biggest and prettiest spread around. Dad says if I still want to next year when I'm sixteen, I can hire out here." His hands firm on the reins, Ben slowed the horse for a turn.

"You really love it, don't you?" Judith marveled.

Ben turned an astonished gaze toward her. "Of course I do. I was born and raised here, Ma'am." His tone said more than his words, and Judith subsided. She couldn't help but see the difference between the Circle S and other places she'd passed.

"Water and care make the difference," Ben said. Had he read her mind? "The Scotts are a hardworking outfit." He brought the light buggy to a stop in front of the house, and Judith noted the courtyard, bright flowers, and plentiful garden.

"Lige? Gideon? You've got comp'ny." Ben jumped down from the driver's seat and courteously helped Joel, who had awakened flushed and curious, and then Judith.

"Where are we, Judy?" Joel wanted to know. He rubbed the sleep from his eyes.

"We're at the Circle S, Dear. It's a big ranch." *That can't be my voice, calm and practical,* Judith thought. *Not when my stomach's going around in circles.*

"Are we going to stay here?" Joel didn't wait for an answer but ran to a nearby rosebush to sniff the flowers. Judith felt reprieved.

"Ben, who is it you've brought us?" A crisp voice with a hint of a Southern accent penetrated Judith's confusion. She turned sharply, and dust sifted from her dress. A woman, whose gray-streaked brown hair shouted middle age but whose slender figure and questioning blue gaze whispered youth, stood near the arched support that held up a wide-roofed porch. Her simple dress of blue calico matched her eyes and fitted her body well. The welcome in her eyes for any stranger reached out to Judith, adrift in a friendless land, unless she counted Pete and Ben.

"I–I am Judith Butler," she began. Her heart pounded. *How can I destroy the peace in this ranch woman's face by informing her of her son's treachery? Or will it all prove to be a terrible case of mistaken identity?* In that moment, Judith fervently hoped so. Better to have made the long trip for nothing than to bring shame to one Judith could have loved as a mother in different circumstances.

"Who are you talking to, Naomi?"

Judith knew she would never forget her first sight of Lige Scott. To her frightened vision, he loomed sky-high and desert-wide. His massive head sat square and proud on strong shoulders. Lige's blue eyes, darkened with some strange and unidentifiable emo-

111

tion, stared at Judith from a network of lines in a range-hardened face. Brown hair predominantly gray successfully told the story of his hardworking life and the fight to get, hold, and expand the Circle S.

"Ben has fetched us a visitor." Naomi smiled and gracefully walked down the steps. "Her name is Judith Butler, but she hasn't told us where she comes from or why she's here."

Lige followed his wife to where Judith stood frozen. If it had seemed impossible to tell Naomi Scott why she'd come, it was preposterous to imagine accusing Gideon to this heavy-browed father. Judith couldn't move. She could not speak. She swayed from weariness, and Ben, openmouthed, steadied her. If only someone would say something, anything, to break this terrible silence before a storm Judith knew would never end.

"Judy, I like it here." Joel deserted the roses, ran from behind the buggy, and stopped between her and the Scotts. "Do you live here? Are we going to stay with you?" he asked.

CHAPTER 7

Oh, God, not like this, Judith silently prayed, despising herself for not speaking. Now it was too late. Innocent, beautiful Joel stood smiling at Naomi and Lige, repeating his question. "Are Judy and I going to stay with you?" The look in his Scott-blue eyes and rosy face showed his eagerness.

Naomi gave a choked cry. Her face turned whiter than cotton. Lige's mighty frame jerked as if someone had shot him. Disbelief turned into anger, then fear on his face. Finally he burst out, *"Dear God in heaven, who are you, Boy?"*

Joel's mouth rounded into a little *o*. He put one finger in his mouth.

Lige fell to his knees before the child and asked again, "Who are you?" Sweat glistened in the furrows of his face.

With the sensitivity of his young years, that strange ability to know when others hurt, Joel's happiness fled. Judith suddenly found her voice. "His name is Joel Scott, Sir."

"No. *No!*" Lige stood and backed away as if pursued. But when Joel's eyes filled and he ran to Judith, the stricken man mumbled, "Forgive me, Boy." He passed one hand over his forehead. "Naomi, take them inside." Before she could comply with his order, Lige glared at the transfixed Ben. "On your way and not a word of this to anyone, you hear?"

"Yes, Sir. I mean, no, Sir." Ben almost fell over himself getting back into the buggy and turning the horse. A cloud of dust followed his rapid progress away from the Circle S and the four left behind to sort out the mystery. Someday Ben might speak of this day, but now all he wanted to do was get away as fast as he would from a threatened rattlesnake.

"Miss Butler?" Naomi Scott regained her composure, although to Judith's excited gaze, she appeared to have aged ten years in the past few moments. "Will you come in, please?" She smiled at the wide-eyed little boy who clung to his aunt's skirts, held by a tension he couldn't understand.

Judith followed the woman into a large hall with a polished dark floor and massive dark furniture. The brightness of Mexico relieved the somber mien: Colorful serapes adorned the cream plaster walls, and matching woven rugs made islands on the waxed floor.

"Oooh, pretty." Joel's love of beauty overcame his temporary shyness. He pointed to an open door leading into the flower-laden courtyard with its splashing fountain.

"Perhaps he would like to go out while we talk," Lige said hoarsely, his gaze fixed on the small boy with a strange intensity Judith couldn't translate.

"May I, Judy?"

"Of course." She hugged him and watched him run into the courtyard before turning to the Scotts. "I apologize for intruding this way, but your son — he —" She swayed and would have fallen if Naomi hadn't caught her arm and led her to a settee. "Child!" The hostess in Naomi rose to the needs of a guest. "Why, you're worn out."

Naomi's kindness threatened to destroy completely what little composure Judith still possessed. "It's such a long way," she faltered. "If I could have a glass of water, please."

Naomi clapped her hands, and a smiling, dark-eyed Spanish woman in a bright, flouncy dress came into the room. "Carmelita, a cool drink for our guest, please."

Before Judith's brain stopped spinning, a tall fruit drink of unknown ingredients, an elixir to restore her spirits, turned the world right side up again.

Aware of Lige's pacing, Judith said, "I didn't want to come here, but I've been sick, and if anything happened to me, there's no one to care for Joel."

"If the boy is really a Scott — and with that face, he can't be otherwise — he will be cared for," Lige interrupted, his anger distorting his features.

Fortified by the drink and spurred by the contemptuous disbelief in Lige's voice, Judith's jaw set and her own anger flared. "Oh, he's a Scott all right."

"You have proof of this?" Naomi asked. Judith had the feeling hope still lived in the woman's heart. "When and where were you married?"

A rush of hot color stained the young woman's smooth cheeks. "Joel is not my son but my half sister's." She then forestalled the inevitable question as to why Millicent hadn't come herself. "Millie died before Joel was even a year old." She fumbled with her reticule. "I've taken care of him since."

"You aren't much more than a child yourself," Naomi observed. "How did you manage?"

116

"I am nineteen, Mrs. Scott." Her level gaze didn't waver. "One does what one has to do." She glanced at Lige and caught a grudging admiration in his big eyes. A moment later, the papers crackled in her fingers, but a strange reluctance made her add, "Would you like to hear the whole story?"

Naomi nodded, but Lige said nothing. Taking his silence as a consent, Judith began with the death of their parents, the unusual closeness between the sisters, and the advent of Gideon who, according to Millie, was every storybook hero rolled into one. "I couldn't understand why he wouldn't meet me," she said. Tears sparkled on her long lashes just remembering that awful time.

"Looking back, it appears he knew he couldn't get Millie any way except by marriage." She ignored a growl of protest from Lige and rushed on. "Anyway, they went away for a brief honeymoon. I'd never seen Millie so happy as when she came back wearing a pale blue dress. She had brought a beautiful gown for me, and we got ready the next morning and waited for her husband to come." Those agonizing hours returned. "He didn't even have the courage to tell Millie all his talk about making a home where I'd always be welcome was just

that, talk. He sent a Negro with a message."
Judith fished it out and read the words
made faint by the years.

A terrible cry burst from Lige, but Judith
knew she must go on. Once told, she never
intended to mention that time again. "Your
son might as well have put a gun to Millie's
heart. Something in her died, perhaps the
will to live. A few months later, she knew
she was with child, and I believe she forgave
everything because of the coming of her
son." Judith quickly sketched in the next
months, culminating with the death of her
half sister.

"She made me promise I would only
search for Joel's father if the time came
when I could no longer care for him."

"But why?" Naomi cried. Her hands
twisted, and the pain in her eyes made Judith look away. "Surely she knew that in
such circumstances . . ." She couldn't go
on.

"She knew her husband's family was well-
to-do and feared Joel might be taken from
her," Judith said in a dull voice. Would her
lagging strength help her finish this ordeal?

"Did my son know about the boy?" Lige
stepped closer. His eyes gleamed.

"I don't see how he could, Sir." Judith felt
pity stir inside her. A man whose pride had

been knifed in the way only a wayward son can do, Lige's big shoulders sagged. "We did everything possible to keep Joel's birth quiet," Judith added.

"Thank God he isn't guilty of more sins," admitted Lige, but his eyes showed that didn't lessen the magnitude of this audacious marriage and desertion. "Did he . . . do you know if he knew of your sister's death?"

Colorless, Judith shook her head. "He had no way of knowing that, I believe, because her death would not have been publicized, and Millie was known to our neighbors as Millicent Greene. When I fell so ill and didn't get my strength back, I knew I had to find him." The same fury assaulted her as when she learned of the effrontery of Millie's cowardly husband by hiding away to become a minister. "It's ironic, but the same means that alerted me to your son's whereabouts elevated him!" She intercepted the blank gaze between the Scotts but continued, "I wrote to him here in San Scipio and told him Millie died in early 1871 and asked him to contact me."

Judith heard the bellow of a terrified bullock that had escaped its master and burst into view not far from where she stood. The rage and pain resembled that in Lige Scott's voice. "Then that's why he — my son, my son!"

"Sir, I can never tell you how sorry I am to come here, but Joel must have someone in case I can't go on." Her low voice echoed in the too-silent room. Spent, Judith leaned back against the cushions of the settee.

"Then our son still doesn't know he has a child?" Naomi inquired. Her face sagged with shame. "Such a beautiful little boy to be fatherless for so many years." She patted Judith's hand. "You were right to come, my dear, although the shock is almost more than can be borne. Elijah, we will open our hearts and home to these orphaned children, both of them."

Before he could reply, two persons simultaneously entered the hall. Joel ran back in from the courtyard, his face lighted with happiness. A tall man with sun-streaked hair and an open face hurried inside. Their paths collided. A last-minute catching of the child in his arms saved Joel from a nasty fall. "Whoa, there, muchacho." The man laughed down into the child's face, then went blank with astonishment. "Why, who are you?" He whirled toward his parents and Judith.

In a sudden motion, Judith sprang to her feet and planted clenched fists on her hips. "You are Gideon Carroll Scott."

He looked amazed and set Joel down. "I don't think I've had the pleasure of meeting you, Miss."

"Nor I you." Judith clenched her teeth. "Joel, Dear, would you go back into the courtyard for just a few minutes more?" She forced a smile.

He sighed, and she knew he sensed the undercurrents that were turning the placid room into a sea of emotion. His feet dragged, and the joy of discovery he'd shown before now was sadly lacking.

"Is something wrong?" A shadow came into the young man's blue eyes. "That child, he looks so much like —"

"Why shouldn't he look like the Scotts?" Judith cried, her nerves strained to the breaking point. "He's *your* son!"

"*What?*" Gideon stepped toward her. "Are you an escaped lunatic?"

"Gideon!" Lige thundered, and Judith observed the profound change in the man. His shoulders squared. Life flowed back into his face and, with it, the darkest fury she had ever seen in a human's face.

"What's this all about?" Gideon demanded. He planted fingers in her shoulders and held fast. "How dare you come here with such a story!"

"Do you deny it?" Judith tore herself from

the cruel grasp.

Gideon's face flamed until he looked like an avenging angel. "Deny it! My dear woman, you must be mad."

She lost control. "Then deny this." She snatched the carefully preserved wedding certificate and thrust it into his face. "Gideon Carroll Scott and Millicent Butler, my half sister, united in holy matrimony, July 29, 1869, in New Orleans. More like unholy matrimony." A sob escaped despite her best efforts. "You married her, carried her off for a few days, then deserted her. Your child was born the following April."

"It's a lie!" Gideon yanked the paper from her hands. His face turned ghastly. "I never even heard of a Millicent Butler, let alone married one. Father, Mother, you don't believe this woman, do you?"

"Do you deny you were in New Orleans at that time?" Judith prodded, while something inside her wished he could.

"Of course not. Cyrus and I were both there. I'd just started studying to be a minister." He looked at the wedding certificate, then started. Color poured into his face, and he squinted and peered again. "This isn't my handwriting, even though it looks like it."

"And I suppose this isn't, either." Judith

produced the farewell note in its dilapidated state.

"I don't understand." Gideon went white to the lips. His eyes blazed like twin coals. Then recognition set in. "There's been a terrible mistake."

Why should her heart leap? What was this stranger to her? Judith's nails dug into her palms until they ached.

"What have you done, Gideon?" Lige marched to his son, his face a mask of stone.

"Why are you so willing to believe that I am guilty?" Gideon shouted. "I tell you, I've never seen this woman or heard of her sister." All the longing of years for his father's approval blended into his cry of despair. "If you want the truth, find Cyrus. It would be like him to marry someone using my name, and he's always been able to imitate my writing."

Crack. Lige's mighty open hand struck his younger son with such power that Gideon staggered. Bright red replaced the white of his left cheek. A suspicion of froth ringed Lige's mouth. "How *dare* you accuse your brother of your wickedness? I won't have it, do you hear?"

Gideon didn't give an inch. His eyes blazed. "Can't you even trust me until I can prove you're wrong? I have no son, and I have had no wife."

Something inside Judith turned over. If ever a voice and face proclaimed the truth, Gideon's did. Uncertainty gnawed at her. Could this young man honestly be the victim of a sadistic joke?

"Judy, are you all right?" Joel's eyes looked enormous, and he raced back inside to his sole source of comfort. "Everyone's yelling. Let's go somewhere else."

Where? rang in her brain, yet she kept her voice quiet. "If someone will drive us back to San Scipio, we'll go away. Perhaps I can find work in El Paso." *If we have money enough to get there,* she thought. Suddenly Pete's weathered face came to mind. Surely he'd help her, lend her enough to go on. Besides, God wouldn't let them down, ever.

"The child stays here." Lige, more in control than ever, belligerently stepped between Judith and the door.

"My Judy, too?" Joel rushed in where angels would have hesitated on the doorstep. He looked anxiously up at Lige.

"Of course." With a visible effort, the tall man tempered his voice. "Boy, do you like horses?"

Joel allowed himself to be sidetracked. "P'r'aps. That's what Judy says I must say when I don't know." His enchanting, in-

124

nocent laugh lightened the atmosphere. He looked around the room, cocked his head at Gideon, and said, "Why do you look at my Judy so? Don't you like her?" He sat down on a stool and put one hand beneath his elbow and his chin on the supported hand. "We came such a long way. But if you don't want us, we have to go."

Naomi gave a little cry and clapped her hands. "We want you very much, Child. You're our own —" She bit off the end of the sentence and called to the maid. "Carmelita, take Miss Butler and Joel to the big room with the alcove." She then explained to Judith, "It has a small bed in the alcove for Joel and a large bed for you. I'll send up hot water immediately. Would you like supper trays instead of coming down tonight?"

Her thoughtfulness, coming so close on the cease-fire of hostilities, left Judith unsteady. "If you'd be so kind. I know Joel is exhausted."

"So are you." Naomi put a strong arm around the frail shoulders that had carried such heavy burdens for so many years. "Don't worry about anything. Whatever has happened is done and not the child's or your fault. You are welcome here, and we will talk later when all of us are less upset. Now go with Carmelita."

It seemed a long walk from the big hall to the airy rooms, but Judith rightfully attributed it to her fatigue. Even Joel acted subdued. Unused to scenes and fiercely loyal to his Judy, the little boy clung to her hand and walked sedately instead of skipping as he normally did. "We don't have to stay," he repeated after Carmelita left them. "It's nice, though." He walked to the window and looked out into the courtyard. "The flowers are pretty. Did God make them?"

"Yes, Dear." Almost too tired to respond, Judith strove to bring a more normal tone into their conversation. Time enough later to sort everything out. First she must bathe Joel, see that he ate, force food into herself, and put her charge to bed. She hadn't counted on Naomi Scott's graciousness. She herself appeared with the maids bearing hot water and supervised the filling of the tub screened off at one end of the room. She then carried Joel to her own quarters, returning later with a rosy boy in place of a dusty one. Naomi remained with them until Joel fell asleep, then personally tucked Judith into an enormous bed, plumped the pillows, and dropped an impulsive kiss on the young woman's forehead.

"Don't worry about a thing." Her gaze

turned toward the worn Bible. "You're a Christian, aren't you?"

"Yes, for all my life."

"I am so glad." Naomi patted Judith's hand, then knelt by the bedside. "Our Father, we thank Thee for the gift of Thy Son. We thank Thee for sending these, Thy precious children, to us. We do not always comprehend Thy ways, but help them to know Thy loving care is around them, and grant them peace and rest. In the name of Thy Son, Jesus. Amen."

When the tears of weakness crowded Judith's eyelids, she simply squeezed Naomi's hand, which rested on hers, and listened for the closing of the massive door. She had thought she would lie awake for hours. Instead, she fell into a deep and dreamless sleep.

Judith awakened at sunrise when a cock crowed. The thick adobe walls shut out the sounds of the house, but through the open window came noises she had come to identify with life in the West. Too tired to care, she gratefully remembered Naomi's admonition to sleep as long as she could. She turned over and closed her eyes again.

"Judy, are you awake?"

She stirred from the fathoms of deep sleep to discover Joel in his nightshirt standing by her bed. Automatically, she scooted over and made room for him. The long rest had done its work well. Today might bring more problems, but at least she had survived the confrontation with Gideon.

Her heart lurched, and again she wondered why she should find it impossible to believe Gideon Carroll Scott's treachery. She considered it with part of her mind while answering Joel's chatter. Connecting such a frank-faced young man, who looked every bit the part of a man who longed to serve his God with his all, with what she knew of Millie's husband and Joel's father took more imagination than she owned. If she hadn't had the marriage certificate, the farewell note, and the young man's face stamped in miniature every time she looked at Joel, Judith could never have believed what had to be true.

"Judy. *Judy!*" Joel shook her arm hard, slid from bed, and ran to the window looking out toward the corral. "Come quick. There's a baby horse looking in our window!"

Almost as excited as the child, Judith dropped her meditations and sped across the large, richly carpeted room. *Dear God,* she prayed, *we've been in some pretty strange places, but this is the first time You've ever led us to one where we wake up and find a horse staring in at us.* Laughing at herself, she hugged Joel and said, "Let's get dressed. Who knows what's next?"

CHAPTER 8

From that first San Scipio sermon, Gideon loved his chosen work. He rode early and late seeking out isolated families, bringing the kind of ministry they most needed: not always a retelling of the gospel, but a living message of Jesus Christ that permitted and encouraged his participation in whatever the family might be doing. Whether rounding up strays, branding cattle, or even digging postholes, the most hated cowboy chore, Gideon had experienced the tasks on the Circle S and was an able helper.

"I never heerd tell o' no preacher doin' sich things," one grandmother protested. "Jest don't seem fittin'."

"Now, Granny." Gideon gave her the smile her Irish grandmother said warmed the cockles of her heart. "Remember how Jesus worked in the carpenter shop? I'll bet if He were to drop in, He wouldn't command you to leave bawling cows that needed herding.

No, He'd take care of the work first, then have words for you of an evening, when the sun's ready to hit the bunk and let the moon have a chance to shine."

"You shore talk purty. Say, Gideon, when're you aimin' to find yourself a gal and git hitched?"

Gideon threw back his head and laughed. Mischief twinkled in his eyes. "Granny, are you proposing to me? Why, I believe you are. You're blushing all over your face."

"Go 'long with you, Gideon Scott. Don't you know a preacher's s'posed to be serious?" she scolded, even though she couldn't help laughing.

Gideon shook his head. "I find a whole lot more places in the Bible where we're told to be glad and rejoice than to go around with a face so long it's in danger of getting stepped on." He warmed to his subject. "When Jesus says He came to bring life and to bring it more abundantly, I believe that included real happiness and laughter. If more folks could see that, more of them would want to follow Christ."

"I plumb agree," the old woman said surprisingly. "There's enough miz'ry in life without it creepin' into religion."

"Good for you, Granny!" Gideon shook her hand, amazed at her hard strength and insight into things eternal. "Tell you what. First time I get to feeling bad, I'll ride back over here and let you preach me a sermon."

"I kin do it, too," she boasted, and her dark eyes sparkled. "How do you think I raised me five fine sons?"

Her question perched on Gideon's saddle horn when he turned the sorrel mare Dainty Bess toward home. Of all the horses on the Circle S, he liked her best, but he saved her for riding and chose heavier stock for working the range. From earliest dawn to last daylight, he rode and roped, talked with his heavenly Father, and prepared down-to-earth, practical sermons suited to the San Scipio area. No lofty sentiments could ease the harshness of life in West Texas in the 1870s. Gideon's prayers that incorporated pleas for today's strength and tomorrow's hope offered his widely scattered and diverse congregation a rope to which they could cling in times of trouble and happiness.

Cyrus's continued absence remained the one thorn in Gideon's side. The young minister had made surreptitious inquiries but so far had run into only dead-end trails. If a tornado had swooped down and clutched Cyrus, his disappearance couldn't have been more complete. Again and again, Gideon prayed for his brother, whose wasted, reckless life lay heavy on Gideon's soul. "Oh, God," he cried a hundred times. "Somehow, make Cyrus see and know how much he needs You." Yet weeks drifted by with no trace of the missing brother.

That one thorn also wedged itself into the new and tenuous relationship Gideon and his father had begun to develop. Gideon spent every spare minute he could find trying in some small way to replace Cyrus. Not in Lige's affections, but merely in working on the Circle S. While he would never be as proficient in range work as the superbly trained Cyrus, the long hours in the saddle plus practicing with rope and gun brought their rewards.

"Seems strange for a preacher to be practicing shooting," he told Lige one late afternoon when he had brought down a hawk threatening the baby chicks Naomi adored.

"God forbid you ever have to use that gun except in times like these." Lige nodded at the downed hawk. His face, which had grown more downcast since Cyrus rode out, turned hard. "You won't always be where you're known and have the backing of friends. Son, when that time comes, remember this: If those who test you know you can shoot and shoot well, chances are you're less likely to have to than if you never packed a gun and relied on being a preacher to protect you."

It was a long speech for his father. Gideon took a deep breath. "Thanks." The word *Dad* hovered on his lips but wouldn't come out. Not since Cyrus left had he felt he could say it, for Lige had returned to the forbidding father figure of childhood.

One morning when Gideon had ridden into San Scipio, Sheriff Collins sought him out. Long and lanky, his soft-spoken way hid iron nerves and sinews. "Heard anything of Cyrus lately?" he asked in his searching drawl.

"Why, no," Gideon said, his heart beating faster. "Have you?"

The sheriff shifted his quid and spat an accurate stream of tobacco juice into the street. "Naw. Just curious as to why he'd ride out so suddenlike." He grinned. "I consider myself a brave man, but I don't plan to ask your daddy about it."

"I don't blame you." A look of understanding passed between them. Gideon decided to lay his cards on the table. "Sheriff, its half killing my father. You know how he is about Cyrus."

"Huh, everybody knows. Rotten shame how blind a man can be when he sets such store in his son and won't hear a thing against him." A heavy hand came down on Gideon's shoulder. "Is there anything I should know?"

"I've racked my brain over and over. All I know is that Cyrus planned to be at the church dedication. Then he rode into town, got some kind of letter, and said he was riding out." Gideon didn't add the part about Cyrus's strange talk, asking Gideon to promise he wouldn't go back on him, forgiving seventy times seven and the like. "All I could figure is that Cyrus had been gambling and someone threatened to come collect. Father hates any kind of betting. Even Cyrus couldn't get away with that." He wrinkled his forehead. "Except if that's true, why hasn't whoever wrote the letter shown up?"

The sheriff glanced both ways. No one lounged within earshot. "Something you ought to know. I saw the envelope. It came from New Orleans."

A rush of blood flowed to Gideon's head. "*New Orleans?* But Cyrus was only there that one time five years ago. He never writes letters, didn't write to me once while I was gone. Who could be trying to contact him after all this time?" The idea troubled Gideon. Surely if Cyrus had been up to his usual tricks, it wouldn't take this long for a cheated or irate gambler to trace him.

Sheriff Collins spat again. "If I were a gambling man, which I ain't, I'd bet that if I could find that letter, some of the mystery might get solved." He grinned companionably at the younger man. "Now, it's none of my affair 'less I get a complaint. Like I said, I'm just interested."

"Thanks, Sheriff." Gideon slowly walked into the general store and made his purchases, absently noting the way Lucinda Curtis bustled around and made a great show of efficiency in waiting on him. He tipped his wide hat politely and backed out, then filled his saddlebags and headed home. *Would it be wrong to search Cyrus's room?* Never had he trespassed on the unwritten law of privacy Lige established between the brothers when they were small. Did the desire to know where Cyrus had gone — and why — warrant breaking this tradition?

Anything that would straighten things out and bring Cyrus back to Lige was justified. Gideon couldn't bear seeing his father turn more and more inward with each passing day. Naomi hadn't expressed her concern verbally, but it showed in her gaze at her husband.

Rejoicing in the thickness of walls that

muffled and silenced movement in other parts of the adobe ranch house, long after every light had been extinguished for the night, Gideon crept into his brother's room. Except for the clothing that Rosa and Carmelita had hung up, nothing in the room showed signs of entry. Gideon forced himself to go through each drawer of the tall chiffonier, each pocket of the clothing in the closet. Not a telltale scrap of paper showed itself. But why should it? Gideon remembered as clearly as if it had been only an hour ago how Cyrus's fingers had strayed to his breast pocket that morning in the courtyard.

"Too bad he didn't change clothes," the searcher muttered. He tried to put things together in sequence. Evidently, Cyrus had received bad news from the letter, yet it had been the night before when he demanded loyalty from his brother! Had Cyrus carried a guilty secret, perhaps for a long time, that he knew would be exposed someday but hadn't expected it to happen so soon? It seemed the only explanation. Either that or a premonition of trouble ahead so strong it forced him to ensure Gideon's support.

Gideon carefully replaced everything he had disturbed in his fruitless search. He also spent a long time praying for Cyrus before he fell asleep.

Several days later, Gideon headed for home in the late afternoon on Dainty Bess. Usually the horse whinnied when he turned her toward the ranch house and corrals, but today she stepped as lightly and smooth gaited as if they had been on the trails for an hour.

"Good girl." Gideon patted her silky mane, then relaxed in the saddle. One of her best qualities was the little guidance she needed, especially on the trail home. Gideon's mind stayed free to pursue his thoughts and dreams. When the mare stopped of her own accord on the mesa above the ranch, Gideon was roused from his comfortable slumped position in the saddle.

"Dust cloud. Wonder who's at the ranch?" Gideon waited to let Bess's heavy breathing from their climb return to normal, then headed down the trail. "It's Ben, from town. He's sure making tracks with that buggy." Gideon raised one eyebrow. The towheaded youngster's driving skill and carefulness beyond his years certainly didn't match the way that horse and carriage pelted away from the Circle S.

Dread filled Gideon. Perhaps someone in town had been hurt or needed him. Or something had happened to Cyrus . . . He touched Dainty Bess with his boot heels, scorning the spurs most cowboys used. "Hi-yi, Ben!" Bess picked up speed and flashed down the winding wagon road toward Ben. Gideon pulled her in short, and Ben stopped his panting horse. "Somebody hurt or dead?" Gideon demanded.

Ben shook his head. "Comp'ny at the ranch."

Why does the boy look so upset? Gideon wondered. A reader of faces, he saw disillusionment, anger, and the desire to get away rise in Ben's eyes. "Is something wrong?"

"Find out for yourself." Ben clucked to the horse and drove off, this time at a pace more fitting for the climb from valley floor to the mesa top.

"Something's sure eating him," Gideon commented and watched the buggy until it turned the bend and slipped out of sight. "First time he hasn't been friendly." He thought of the faithful way Ben and other young people came to church and of the high hopes he held for their salvation. He knew Ben had accepted the Lord in his heart, but so far he hadn't made it public. Gideon knew he would wait until the Holy Spirit did its work, so he didn't push.

Besides, boys like Ben — and the way he'd been at fifteen — had to be *led* to the Master, never driven.

In spite of his eagerness to discover who Ben had delivered to the ranch and why it upset the boy, Gideon rubbed Dainty Bess down and watered her before going into the house. He hesitated on the cool porch, held for a moment by the same feeling he'd experienced those times before a storm. Silence, ominous and threatening, filled him with a reluctance to step across the threshold into the big hall.

To make up for his anxiety, he hurried inside, his long steps eating up the polished floor. A small blue and white and gold whirlwind raced in front of him. Unable to stop his momentum, Gideon snatched up the little boy and held him with strong arms. "Whoa there, muchacho." First he laughed, but then as he peered into the child's eyes, he felt the blood drain from his face. "Why, who are you?" He turned toward his parents. A strange young woman exploded from a settee and planted clenched fists on her hips. Travel-stained and dusty, with dark brown eyes that matched her coiled, braided hair, she glowed with an unearthly light. "You are Gideon Carroll Scott."

How could five simple words carry so

much hatred and reproach? Gideon mumbled something and put down the child, who slowly went into the courtyard at the stranger's bidding. Who was she, and who was the child who looked enough like the Scotts to be one?

Ice water trickled in his veins. "Is something wrong?" Gideon asked. "That child, he looks so much like —"

Then it came. The squall Gideon had known lay waiting behind the closed ranch house door. "Why shouldn't he look like the Scotts?" Beautiful in her scorn, the young woman faced and indicted him. "He's your son."

The room spun. *Is the woman mad?* An eternity of accusations followed, along with a wedding certificate bearing his name. *Dear God, this can't be happening!* Gideon turned to his parents for comfort. *They can't believe this preposterous claim, can they?* His heart turned to a lead ball and sank to his boots. Lige believed the charge. It showed in every terrible twitch of his shaken body.

"This isn't my handwriting." He tried to defend himself. The girl produced a second piece of evidence, and light broke. *Cyrus.* Cyrus, who would stop at nothing to get what he wanted and leave others to bear the blame and shame. A flash of insight solved the strange pleas for seventy times seven forgiveness. *No, God, not this time. Let Father see what his precious older son has done.*

Gideon cried out his defense and received a blow that bruised his face but cut into his heart. Even the flicker of doubt in the woman's eyes when he proclaimed his belief that Cyrus had done this couldn't change a father's loyalty to one son at the expense of another. The temper Gideon had inherited but tried to control blazed. "Can't you even trust me until I can prove you're wrong? I have no son, and I have had no wife!" Again uncertainty showed in the watching dark eyes. Then the child called Joel ran back, frightened, needing reassurance. Gideon couldn't move, not when the stranger said they would go. Not when Lige protested. Not even when Joel asked with childish perception, "Why do you look at my Judy so? Don't you like her?" Only when Carmelita led the visitors away did strength return to Gideon's limbs and free him from the paralysis of shock.

"Father, I have never asked much from you, but I ask you now. Do you honestly believe that I am capable of marrying a woman, then deserting her?" Gideon knew his future hung in the balance. He saw doubt rise in his father's eyes. He saw the massive head begin to shake from side to side and the mouth form the word, "No." Then a transformation killed the final hope struggling for life in the young minister's breast. His mouth tasted the ashes of dishonor placed on an innocent man.

"The child is a Scott." Lige's sonorous voice rolled his verdict into the hall, where it hung in the air.

"I am not the only Scott who lived in New Orleans in the summer of 1869," Gideon said rashly, as if pouring kerosene on the fire of Lige's reactions.

"Only a sniveling coward puts blame on a man who is not here to defend himself," Lige bellowed. He raised his hand to strike again the son who dared accuse his favorite.

"No, Elijah!" Naomi planted herself squarely in front of her enraged husband. "We have never known Gideon to lie." Magnificent in her rare opposition to the lord of the household, she held him at bay in defense of her man-child. "There is more to this than we know. I feel that. Until we find the truth, we will keep the child and the young woman here."

"The truth? Woman, what more evidence do you want than a marriage certificate in your son's writing —" Gideon winced at the words *your son,* but Lige went on. "Also

143

a note and the child himself!" Suspicion blackened his face. "Or are you also accusing Cyrus?"

"I am accusing *no one,* despite what you call evidence." Naomi didn't give an inch. Her face the color of parchment, her blue eyes shone with the fire of motherhood roused on behalf of her young. Gideon's cold heart warmed. All the adoration and love the lonely little boy had poured out on Naomi when denied his father's affection paled into insignificance when compared with what he felt for her now.

"Someday I will prove what I say is true," he promised. Before either could reply, Gideon turned on his heel and went out, his steps echoing in the hall. *How? How? How?* they mocked.

By finding Cyrus. The answer came sharp and bright as a lightning flash. He must leave San Scipio, find his brother, and for the first time in his life, force Cyrus to take the consequences of his actions.

Gideon's lips twisted bitterly in sharp contrast to their usual upward tilt. Father would rage and fume, but in the end, he'd be so glad to have his object of adulation back, the anger would dwindle and vanish. The presence of a grandson's softening influence would finish the job. Lige would cling to the boy as a second Cyrus.

"Father will also probably coerce Cyrus into marrying the woman," Gideon whispered into Dainty Bess's mane when she came at his whistle. "God forbid! Any woman who marries Cyrus will be in torment, especially one as untouched and frail as she." Yet what else could she do? Her gown bore mute witness of poverty. Her eyes showed she would never have sought out Joel's father unless she had come to the limits of her strength and ability to care for her nephew. How old was she? Eighteen? Twenty? She had cared for four-year-old Joel when little more than a child herself.

Respect stirred within him. Although he hated what she had done to his life with her false accusation, how could he help but admire a plucky girl who had become a mother by necessity? Gideon thought of the look in her eyes when she first announced him as Joel's father, something she obviously believed. Never before had he seen reflected in anyone's face the belief that he was despicable, beyond contempt.

His jaw squared. "Dear God," he breathed and swung into the saddle for a healing ride, forgetful of the fact he hadn't eaten since breakfast. "Any man who would do what she believes I did to her sister deserves that look." Shame for Cyrus and the passionate wish his brother had been different rose into a crescendo of protest. "Someday, somehow, with Your help, I'm going to prove to Father and to her I am innocent!"

Yet a jeering voice so real it rang in Gideon's ears and beat into his tired brain continued the measured cadence begun by his boot heels in the hall. Over and over the questions *How? How? How?* tormented him until he thought he would go mad.

CHAPTER 9

In the mysterious way Noami had always used to calm her stubborn, volatile husband, she again prevailed. Lige's first decision to disclaim Gideon as his son fell before her reason. While Gideon and Dainty Bess spent the night outdoors and an emotionally exhausted Judith slept soundly, Naomi's quiet voice and Lige's rumbling continued. Shortly before dawn, Naomi fell into a restless sleep, but Lige addressed Almighty God. Hadn't God put fathers in control of their sons? he reasoned. The Bible offered countless examples of what happened when those fathers allowed wickedness to creep into their homes. Lige therefore told God what he planned to do to straighten out the mess, then fell asleep justified.

For the sake of bright-faced Joel, whose winning ways had already softened Lige's stern outlook on life, all discussion was held in abeyance until Carmelita took the boy to the kitchen, where Rosa welcomed him with a smile and a hug. Lige waved the family into a small sitting room. "I have considered this whole unpleasant matter," he began.

Gideon made a sound of protest that died in his throat when his father glared at him. He glanced at Judith, white-faced and still. *How horrible this must all be for her,* he thought. First the long, tiring trip, then a plunge into confusion. Although she admitted she had slept, dark circles still haunted her eyes.

"Your mother has requested that I wait to pass final judgment on your actions." Lige's stony face showed doing so went against everything he believed. "Very well. You say Cyrus is somehow involved, which of course is impossible, but I will give you one month to see if you can locate and bring him back to the Circle S." A world of longing tinged his words. "Miss Butler, according to your story, you sent a letter to Gideon?"

The accused minister could keep silent no longer. "I never received a letter, but when Cyrus said he was leaving, he had a letter in his pocket." Gideon ignored Naomi's warning look. "Sheriff Collins in town said he saw a letter from New Orleans."

"Sheriff Collins?" Lige's face turned purple. "You dared discuss Cyrus with *him?"*

"Father, he asked where Cyrus had gone and brought up seeing the letter."

Cunning and pride resulted in Lige barking, "And did he say he saw the name of the person the letter was addressed to?"

Gideon's heart sank, knowing which turn the conversation had taken. "No."

"See?" Lige turned triumphantly to his wife. "Miss Butler's letter, if this were it, obviously came to Gideon."

"Then why did Cyrus open it?" Gideon demanded. "You trained us from the cradle that a sealed letter to another family member was not to be tampered with."

Lige shrugged. "Perhaps the seal had been broken."

"Then why didn't Cyrus just give me the message? Why did he ride away and say he might never come back?"

"I am not on trial here," Lige roared. "Neither is your brother. Before God, if it were not for your mother, you'd be sent packing." The veins in his neck became cords, pulsing with angry blood. "Gideon Carroll Scott, I offer you a month, for the sake of Naomi's pleading. If by that time you haven't proved to my satisfaction your innocence in this affair, San Scipio will know of your guilt. That is my promise."

Any chance of ever proving Cyrus guilty to his father seemed slim. Yet a month could change much. "I will leave today." Gideon stood, and his mouth set in a straight, grim line.

"Remember, one month. Not a day longer." The judgment followed Gideon when he stepped into the hall. Yet he was not to leave the ranch without one more disturbing interview. An hour later, he had packed what he needed, saddled Dainty Bess, and bade his mother good-bye. Lige had ridden out after delivering his ultimatum without another word to his son. Torn between what lay ahead and had been, Gideon lightly mounted Bess.

"Wait, oh, please, wait!" Judith ran toward him, casting a furtive glance back at the house. She obviously didn't want to be observed. Her dark eyes caught gleams from the sun, and she looked distraught. "Mr. Scott, I don't see how you can be innocent, but if I have falsely accused you — if indeed this brother has used your name — I hope you find him."

The unexpectedness of her seeking him out left Gideon speechless.

She stepped closer and peered up into his face. "Good-bye, Mr. Scott. May God —"

She broke off as if not knowing what to say to him.

"Miss Butler, even if I can never prove it, I am not guilty in spite of the apparent evidence against me. Do you believe me?" Suddenly it seemed imperative that she do so.

"I don't know. It doesn't seem possible that you, a minister of God . . . you seem so honest and yet . . ." Her voice trailed off.

"I thank you for coming out here," he said softly. Then he touched Dainty Bess with his heels and rode away, not looking back but still able to see the troubled girl with her dark eyes that tried to look into his very soul.

Judith's slight change of manner toward him raised his spirits. So did the long, impassioned prayer he made near a big rock off the trail a few miles from the Circle S. "Dear God, You know I am innocent. You know I have no way to prove it. Your power can open doors I don't even know are there. You can uplift me and lead me to Cyrus. Surely this is why he ran away."

Gideon determinedly put aside what could happen if he caught up with his brother. By some means, Cyrus must be made to return to the ranch and clear his brother's name. Yet as the days flew into a week, then another, doubts clouded the searcher's mind. He could not find a trace of Cyrus. What if all these weeks he had lain somewhere in the canyons or over a precipice, the victim of an accident or foul play? The thought whitened Gideon's lips. He hadn't even considered such a thing, but now it seemed highly possible. Cyrus often consorted with evil men who knew he liked to carry money on him. Why hadn't he thought of such a thing before?

"Because of the way he left," Gideon told Dainty Bess. "He planned to go for some unnamed reason. I believe Judith Butler's letter forced his hand."

More days passed. By the end of the third week, Gideon daily stormed heaven. "Dear heavenly Father, ever since I gave my heart to You, I've tried to follow in the footsteps of Your Son. Where are You now? I need to find Cyrus. Only You know where he is. Why aren't You leading me to him?" Always after such a prayer, the young minister experienced pangs of guilt, but low anger also rose. He read the Bible, noted the promises, and prayed again.

Sometimes he wondered if the prayers even got beyond the wide sky above him. Bitterness as acrid as the alkali water he found in distant water-holes seeped into his soul. Was this how the Israelites felt when they wandered in the desert? Forsaken, deserted, and so alone they could barely go on?

Miles from the ranch with a few days left, Gideon turned back. He had considered vanishing the way Cyrus had done, but he rejected it as the coward's way out. Once more he would stand before his father and ask for mercy and trust. If Lige withheld it, Gideon would turn Dainty Bess back to the trails, never to return home.

From the moment Gideon disappeared from sight, a time of waiting began for the Circle S, especially for Judith. She often wondered what strange impulse had caused her to seek out the young man with the sun-streaked hair and starlight in his blue eyes. At times she prayed for him in a stumbling manner that reflected her troubled mind. On one hand, there was the written evidence; on the other, there was the spirit of a man who looked into her eyes and pledged his innocence. Like a weather vane subject to each change of wind, so Judith veered from disbelief to a wavering acceptance of Gideon, the minister, as compared with Gideon, husband and father. Then again, the very beauty of his face could be what deceived Millie so thoroughly. Judith grew weary thinking of it.

In those waiting days and weeks, Joel, however, thrived as never before. Besides the love Naomi and Lige had for their new grandson, the good food and fresh autumn air bolstered the joyful child. The "baby horse" that had peeked in the window that first morning became Joel's own. In a specially designed saddle Lige proudly said he had fashioned when Cyrus was small, Joel jounced and bounced around the corral pulled by a lead rope and loved every minute. He lost some of his toddler chubbiness and gained a tanned complexion from endless hours outdoors.

"Judy, are we going to stay here f'rever and f'rever?" he anxiously asked one day when they sat together in a porch swing.

"Do you like it here that much?" She held her breath, almost hating to hear the answer she knew would come.

"Oh, yes!" His twin sapphire eyes glowed. "Gramma and Gran'pa and Rosa and Carm'lita's so nice." His joy dimmed, and he scooted closer to her. "Don't you like it, too?"

"I love it." She felt his little wiggle of joy. "I just don't know if the Scotts w–want me."

Judith hated herself for the break in her voice.

Joel climbed into her lap. "Don't be sad, Judy." He stroked her now rounded cheek, a result of proper food and freedom from responsibility. "Gran'pa says if you and Gideon get married, everything will be all right."

"What?" She set the child farther out on her knees so she could look directly into his face. "Joel, are you making that up?"

His sensitive lips quivered. "I don't tell stories, Judy. You said God doesn't like it."

She could still scarcely believe his childish gossip. "I know, Dear, but think very hard. Did Mr. Scott really say what you told me?"

He nodded vigorously until his blond curls bounced. Anxiety still filled his eyes. "That's 'zackly what Gran'pa said. Don't you want to marry Gideon?"

"I barely know him," she retorted, then hugged Joel hard. "Don't worry about it." But she sensed the resistance in him.

"Judy, you wouldn't ever go away and leave me, would you? Not even here." He slid down from her lap and leaned against her arm. "I heard Gramma say her boy went away and left her. Not Gideon. Another boy."

"I won't leave you," she promised. Yet deep inside, the thought formed, *If this is*

what Elijah Scott has in mind, how can I stay?
Once the hateful idea had been so carelessly
planted, Judith felt on edge. She caught the
appraising looks Lige gave her now and then
and appreciated the way Negro slaves must
have felt on the auction block. *Sold to the
highest bidder! Given in marriage to appease
a powerful man who thought he could play
God!* In her thoughts, Judith bitterly paro-
died an imaginary auctioneer.

Her turmoil continued. She wanted to ask
Naomi about the diabolical plan, but she
dared not. There had been no word from
Gideon in the days and weeks he had been
gone, and such talk would upset her more.
If Naomi knew and approved of the plan,
the seeds of trust growing between them
would be permanently thwarted; if she
didn't approve, how long could she hold
out against the driving force of her husband?
If only Gideon would return with Cyrus!
Night after night, Judith prayed for it to
happen. Nothing could be worse than this
prolonged silence, not knowing what might
happen next, now that Joel had innocently
betrayed Lige's scheme.

The charming San Scipio area and the
Circle S offered as a respite a variety of
places to ride. Judith soon outgrew the
capabilities of the gentle horse assigned to

her and took on a trustworthy but more spirited pinto named Patchwork. By the time Joel and his pony graduated from the corral to short rides near the ranch, Judith had already explored much of the surrounding countryside. Autumn frosts had wielded their paintbrushes and left behind brilliant colors in the hills and valleys, mesas, and the deeper canyons. Joel loved to roll in piles of leaves whipped off the trees by capricious winds, but only after Judith had carefully stirred them to make sure no snakes lurked in their depths. At times, when she could put aside her fear of the future, Judith found herself laughing as she hadn't done since Millie died.

"I like you when you laugh," Joel told her solemnly, and she realized that through the years, even her best efforts to keep cheerful for him hadn't been a complete success. Now, although the strain of Gideon's return remained, the freedom given her by Naomi and Lige and the servants' eagerness to watch Joel had left its mark. Judith's favorite place to ride was the mesa top above the valley because it offered the widest view for miles around. Near the end of the fateful month of Gideon's grace, Judith found she paused there often, looking for the dust clouds that heralded riders. A few times they came, but Gideon didn't.

On the morning of the thirtieth day, Lige laid down his breakfast fork. Judith had long since learned to rise when the Scotts did and earn her keep and Joel's by working as a daughter of the house, although she was gruffly told it wasn't necessary. Joel usually awakened then, too, but this particular day, Judith had left him sleeping in his alcove.

"You know what day it is." Lige's voice sent shivers up Judith's spine that intensified when she saw that same look she had observed before, when he appeared to be measuring her.

"We know, Lige." Naomi smiled and passed freshly made apple butter to Judith for the hot biscuits Carmelita brought in. "It will be nice to have Gideon home again." She calmly ate the scrambled eggs still on her plate. "Folks have been wondering why the business you sent him on is taking so long."

Judith choked and buried her face in her napkin. When she emerged, Carmelita had gone back to the kitchen and Lige sat staring at his wife, then glanced meaningfully at Judith. She murmured a hasty, "Excuse me, please, I think I hear Joel," and escaped.

After she had helped him dress and sent him to Rosa for breakfast, she slipped out, saddled her horse as she had learned to do, and rode slowly away from the ranch. Patchwork danced a bit but settled down to her quiet command, "Steady there, Girl." The now-familiar track to the mesa top invited her, and once there, she scanned each direction. Relief filled her. No riders. Yet the day had only begun, and hours would pass before the stroke of midnight.

Twice again that day Judith saddled and rode to the mesa. Once she saw Lige's mighty horse ahead of her, and she rode behind concealing bushes until he had gone. The second time, in early evening, her sporadic vigil paid off. Dust clouds in the early blue dusk hid whoever made them, but Judith's heart thudded. Suddenly afraid of the next minutes and hours, she raced back to the corral, hastily unsaddled, left Patchwork to the ministrations of one of the hands, and ran into the house.

"There are dust clouds on the road from town. I couldn't see who or how many. . . ." She couldn't bear the unreadable expression on Lige's face, the open apprehension that shone in Naomi's eyes. "I must change my clothing." She managed a shaky smile at Joel, who sat on his grandmother's lap holding a picture book.

Why had she ever thought the waiting

hard, she marveled while bathing, then donning a clean dress. Naomi had wasted no time in helping her nearly destitute guest sew a few simple house gowns and one dark dress suitable for church. Judith smoothed the pale green folds, then more firmly anchored her coronet of braids. At least the wanderer would return to a well-groomed houseguest instead of a travel-worn visitor. The irrelevant thought brought color to her face.

Before she got to the big hall the family used most often in the evenings, now warmed by logs in the enormous fireplace against the ever-colder nights, Judith peered out a window that overlooked the front of the house. Dainty Bess, a horse more worn than any she had seen, stood with drooping head. Judith then fixed her gaze on the matching figure who slid from the saddle and buried his face in the horse's mane before leading her to the corral. The fruitless journey showed in the sagging shoulders and slow steps. Judith strained her eyes, desperately hoping to see a second horse, a second tired figure, and turned away stunned to realize how disappointed she felt that Gideon had come back alone.

She slipped into the warm room, and Joel ran to her. Together they curled into a massive chair, where Judith's filmy gown made a splash of light against the tapestry. The atmosphere felt thick enough to cut. Dreading the moment when Gideon would come in, she nevertheless wanted to see him. At least the uncertainty would end.

With slow steps dragging from fatigue, Gideon faced his father, his judge. Gone forever was the boyish face Judith remembered. In its place was a strange countenance whose tired body still carried a dignity of its own that could not be denied, except by the one who refused to see it.

"Well?" Lige's question snapped like a whip.

"I couldn't find Cyrus."

"The month is up." Relentless, unforgiving, and self-righteous, Lige Scott folded his arms across his mighty chest. "I have done what your mother asked. Now you will do what I command."

Naomi ran to her son and wordlessly embraced him. Judith saw in her a beaten woman, at least for now. Yet she released Gideon, clapped her hands sharply, and waited until Carmelita came in. "Please take Joel to his room."

"Yes, Señora." Joel ran to her, and they disappeared. Childish laughter mixed with Carmelita's natural joy drifted back, but the lines in Lige's face did not soften.

"I have considered what God would have me do," he announced.

Judith wanted to shriek. *God! When have you ever listened to God?* Every prayer she had heard him make since she arrived was telling God how things would be, a kind of after-the-plans-formed courtesy.

"Considering all the circumstances and knowing that even as God condemned Eli for not controlling his sons, so shall he not spare fathers who permit wickedness in their family, I offer you two choices." He hesitated, and the world stood still.

"The first is to confess your sins before your congregation, to repent and seek God's forgiveness, mine, and then the people's. If they will accept it, you may continue shepherding the flock."

"You ask this of *me?*" Gideon threw off all evidence of weariness. "To stand before my people and *lie?* Father, how can you?"

Judith thrilled to his final stand for justice, but Lige's answer cut into her thoughts like a knife through a ripe peach. "It is no lie." His mighty fist crashed down on the table before him. "You had your chance to prove the falsehood against your brother. Will you accept this penance?"

"Never!" Gideon drew himself to full

stature. "I have never lied, and I never will to save my reputation or my life."

A curious look of — was it relief? — crept into Lige's eyes. "There is a second way. The child's future must be assured. You will marry Miss Butler, become the father to Joel you should have been for years, and take the place on the Circle S of the brother you so mysteriously drove away." Lige's thundering voice cracked on the last words.

CHAPTER 10

At first his father's outlandish suggestion of marriage didn't register with Gideon. His brain focused on the shocking accusation that he had been responsible for Cyrus leaving. A coldness that matched West Texas in January blanketed him. The next moment, he went white-hot, grasping the full significance of Lige's decree. But before he could respond, Judith sprang up to confront her host.

"How *dare* you play God and dispose of your son's and my lives like this?" she cried. Gideon thrilled at her courage. "You think forcing us to marry will solve everything?" Her ragged laugh reminded Gideon of a dull saw pulled through hardwood. "I know nothing of this son Cyrus who ran away, but the more I hear of him, the more I believe it's possible he did just what Gideon said, married Millie under an assumed name to cover his wicked —"

"Hold your tongue, Miss Butler. You are in no position to say what will or won't be in this household." The normal timbre of his voice added a deadliness his wildest ragings never achieved. "A grandfather's claim to Joel will outweigh yours, especially when I can give the boy everything and you are obviously penniless and dependent on charity." An unpleasant smile under raised shaggy eyebrows drove home his point more clearly than the threat.

"You couldn't be so cruel as to take Joel." Judith knew she fought against terrible odds. "I wish to God I had never let you know of Joel's birth. Better for us both to have starved in New Orleans or even for him to have been taken from me than to know he must live where every thought is controlled." Her eyes blazed. "And you call yourself a follower of the meek and lowly Jesus!" The rasping laugh came again.

"Elijah Scott, I am ashamed of you." Naomi took Judith in her arms. "If you drive this girl away — and your *second* son — I will also leave and take Joel."

"Mother!"

"Naomi!"

Gideon and Lige's exclamations blended. Disbelief gave way to knowledge. Naomi Scott meant every word she said. Her set face showed this was no careless thrust meant to hold her husband at bay. She looked at him over Judith's shoulder. "I mean it, Elijah."

"You, too, would desert me?" His face worked, an awful thing for Gideon to behold. Once he had witnessed a beaver dam crack, crumple, and fall before a relentless, flood-swollen stream. Now his father evidenced the same signs.

"First Cyrus, then Gideon, and now Naomi. What have I done to deserve such misery?" Stubborn to the end, it was apparent he could see no wrong in himself.

Gideon couldn't stand any more. His father had been driven to the dust by phantoms real and imagined, by an unreal pride in his elder son and utter faithlessness in his younger. Gideon licked dry lips and with pounding heart said, "Miss Butler, will you do me the honor of becoming my wife?"

He hadn't thought Judith could turn more pale. From the shelter of his mother's arms, Judith whipped around and stared at him. "No, oh, no!"

"Wait," he implored, conscious of Lige's open mouth and the way Naomi's arms dropped from Judith's shoulders. "It will be an empty contract shoved down our throats for Joel's sake. I knew when I came back unable to prove my innocence, I could never stay on the Circle S. God has allowed me to stand guilty in the eyes of the world and of San Scipio when they learn of this affair." He laughed bitterly. "Well, I'm through trying to preach and lead people to a God I can't trust. I'm riding away. Miss Butler, you won't be troubled with the presence of a husband, even one in name only. Don't answer now, just think about it." He turned to Lige. "Will that suit you?"

Stricken dumb by Gideon's shocking capitulation, Lige mumbled, "No need to ride off if you marry."

"There's every need," Gideon contradicted and felt his chest swell. "I wouldn't even consider such a thing if I planned to stay." He glanced at Judith, marble white and still. "Take what time you need before you answer."

"Even if she should agree, how can you accomplish this?" Naomi's eyes reflected all the doubts he felt but shoved back in favor of necessity.

"You three and Joel can go by stage to El Paso. I'll start ahead of you with Dainty Bess. We'll find a justice of the peace, and once the ceremony's over —" He shrugged, and his mouth twisted. "You'll return here, and the happy bridegroom will ride north

167

or west or anywhere on earth that leads away from San Scipio."

Lige's stunned brain came to life. "What's to prevent you riding on and not meeting us in El Paso?"

Gideon couldn't believe what he heard. If he needed further proof his father didn't trust him, he had it in that one sentence. "It's hardly likely I'd suggest marriage if I didn't intend to be there, is it?" He swept aside any chance for an answer. "Miss Butler, just let me know if you'll be willing. I won't interfere with your life. After I'm gone for a time, you'll have no problem providing grounds for an annulment." He threw his shoulders back and walked out, little caring where he went. Had he been loco to propose marriage to this stranger? He shrugged. Why not? God wouldn't send a helpmeet for a minister whose faith had gone sour, a God who turned deaf ears to His follower's cries for help and left him to bear the stain of a sin not his own.

For three days and nights, Gideon spent little time at the ranch. He gave Dainty Bess a long rest and rode Circle S horses from early to late. He pilfered food from the kitchen after Rosa and Carmelita had finished for the day and avoided meals with the family. He grieved at the look in his mother's eyes, went out of his way to keep his distance from Lige, and hardened his heart against young Joel, who trotted after him. He observed Judith only from a distance. A few times he caught her dark and troubled gaze on him, but he only tipped his sombrero and walked on.

The fourth morning, early, he noted with satisfaction the toss of Bess's head that showed her eagerness to be out of the corral and back on the trail with her master. She came at his whistle, and he stood with one hand on her mane, his face toward the west. "It won't be long, old girl," he promised. She softly nickered and lipped the oats he held in his hand.

"Mr. Scott?"

Gideon turned. He hadn't heard Judith come up behind him. "Yes?" His muscles tensed. Something in her voice set blood racing through him.

"I–I have thought about your proposal." The rising sun lent color to her smooth cheeks and flicked golden glints into her dark coiled braids. Her hands lay clasped in front of her simple workdress. "For Joel's sake, if you meant what you said about going away and this not being a real marriage, I accept." Color richer than from the sunrise flowed into her face. "I never intended to marry, so it will impose no hardship on me to bear your name." Anguish filled her eyes. "I cannot face life without Joel, and as your father said, I have no way to care for him."

Filled with sudden pity, Gideon dared touch her hand for a moment only. "Look, Miss Butler . . ."

"Judith."

"Judith." He took a deep breath. "If the idea of this contract is repulsive to you in any way, we won't go through with it. I'll help you fight Father for the right to keep Joel and see that you find work somewhere." He watched the glad surprise that lightened her countenance give way to reality.

"I've gone over and over everything," she said simply. "I can't take the chance of falling ill again. Neither can I stay on the Circle S unless we marry, as your father wishes." Her slim shoulders shook, then squared. "I suppose in his place, I might feel the same." She managed a little smile. "It's too bad, Mr. Scott. In other circumstances, perhaps we could even have been friends."

"Then you believe in me a little?" It suddenly seemed more important than anything else in the world.

"A little."

Something within Gideon released its painful grip on his heart. He caught her hands. "Judith, if the time ever comes that I can prove my innocence, may I come back? I'm not asking any more of you than what we've agreed on," he hastily added when color rose to her hairline. "Since God has forsaken me, I need to have a dream."

"God never forsakes us, Gideon." She looked earnestly into his eyes. "Right now it seems that way to you, but no matter where you ride, remember, He's there."

He started to speak, to protest and deny, but Judith said, "Perhaps one day you will return, absolved of guilt." Her voice dropped to a whisper. "Shall we tell your fath— your parents?"

"Yes." He released her hands and followed her into the house.

Less than a week later, Judith Butler and Gideon Carroll Scott were married in a dusty El Paso office by a justice of the peace who mumbled what should have been beautiful words. Gideon thought he would scream. What a far cry from the joyous weddings he had performed! When he looked at the young woman beside him, however, an excitement he hadn't counted on shook him to his carefully polished boots. How beautiful she looked in a soft yellow and white gown, yet how little he knew of its past. Joel innocently repeated Judith's explanation

171

about the dress.

"Judy said it came with us from New Orleans," Joel marveled. "In the bottom of the trunk. Mama brought it to Judy even before there was me, when she came home from getting married. Isn't it funny?" Pearly white teeth and a laugh like chiming bells made Joel roll with mirth. "Now Judy's getting married in the very same dress."

Had she worn it to test him? Gideon wondered. If he really had married Millicent, surely he would recognize the gown. Curse Cyrus! Not only had Cyrus ruined his opportunity to minister in San Scipio, he had blotted out all chances for a normal life. What would it be like to have Judith as his real wife, to ride and laugh and love and serve with him? The scales dropped from Gideon's inner vision. He stared at Judith and missed some of what the justice of the peace was droning.

He loved her. Of all the girls in the world, how could God allow him to meet and marry Judith Butler, whose best efforts at comforting him only came to trusting and believing in him a little?

"Place the ring on her finger and repeat after me," the official ordered.

Gideon obediently took the slim hand in his and slid on the plain gold ring he had

172

purchased in El Paso. "I, Gideon, take thee, Judith . . ." A sudden longing to take her and ride away to a place where they could build a new life with Joel left him weak with longing, regret, and a renewed anger at Cyrus. He finished his vows, heard her low responses, and felt her hand tremble in his. Caught up in the desire for his marriage to be more than an empty contract, when the justice of the peace said, "You may kiss your bride," Gideon bent and kissed Judith full on the lips.

"Oh!" Reproach crept into her eyes, red to her face.

"Must a man apologize for kissing his wife?" Gideon recklessly whispered. Spurred by the knowledge that he was about to ride away forever, he kissed her a second time, then hurried her away from the curious eyes of the amazed witnesses. Once outside, he swung into the saddle and picked up the reins.

"Gideon, when are you coming home?" Joel called from the circle of Judith's arms.

"I don't know." His heart ached. Somehow he couldn't say the word *never*. "Father, Mother, good-bye."

Naomi's steady gaze never left her son's. "Vaya con Dios." *Go with God.*

Gideon looked at his father, stunned to

see him nodding, silently adding his bene-
diction. Last of all, he turned sideways in
the saddle and faced Judith. The red lips he
had kissed moved in a wordless farewell,
and something in her eyes flickered, an
expression he could not describe or understand.

In another moment, he would bawl like a
heifer stuck in a thicket. To cover the love
he knew must be shining from his face, Gideon mockingly called, "Good-bye, Mrs.
Scott," and pressing his heels into the
horse's sides, rode away. His added words,
"God keep you, my darling," were lost in
the clatter of his horse's hooves and died
undelivered in the dusty air.

The tumbleweed trail swallowed Gideon as
it had swallowed hundreds of pioneers
before him. Old, young, wicked, misunder-
stood, restless, and driven, they thronged
west, away from homes and families. They
were a breed apart in a land that cared less
about a man's past than what he would
become.

Into this new world that made West Texas
look tame by comparison rode Gideon,
tormented by God's failure to help him and
his new love for a wife he could never claim.
In lonely campfires, he saw her smile;

sunrise on the water brought back the dawning day when she said she would marry him. Her dark eyes stared at him from every shady trail, and her spirit rode beside him until he sought out the company of others, no matter how undesirable, to drive away memories. In the wasteland between sleep and waking when no man can control his thoughts, Gideon dreamed of a day when he could go back honorably. He awakened, haunted by the realization he had nothing to offer her even if he proved Cyrus's guilt and cleared his own name. Judith had miraculously retained her deep faith in God through everything life dealt her, whereas he, a minister, had not. His broken faith and corroding soul could never be "equally yoked" with Judith's unswerving faith.

A hundred times he told Dainty Bess, "If only things had been different, what a minister's wife she would be!" He often felt guilty for marrying her, although she had asserted she had no interest in marriage. Suppose she met someone who changed her mind? Would she feel bound by those mumbled vows and give up a chance for happiness? He writhed, jealously cringing at the thought of Judith as another man's wife.

Weeks later, he rode into the mining

country of Colorado through snow that clogged the horse's hooves and slowed them until he wondered if they could make it. His present apathy left him caring little for his own life, but he pressed on because of his faithful horse. Bess deserved better than death in a blizzard because her cowardly owner holed up and froze. Now at the bottom of his stores of flour, beans, and rice, and without hope of finding fresh meat, blood rushed into his face when he reached to the very bottom of his saddlebag and found a small sack. "What on earth —" Gideon stared at the contents. *Money.* His cold, bewildered brain couldn't understand. Had some outlaw who crossed his trail and shared his grub left it there, a rude payment for kindness, stolen from some bank?

Suspicion crystallized and became belief. The odd look in Lige's face, especially just before he rode away from El Paso, provided the answer. Had Father carefully hidden the money, knowing Gideon would only find it when he had exhausted his reserves?

From despair to renewed determination, Gideon knew now he would go on. He would search and find Cyrus or somehow make the folks back home proud, the folks and Judith. For the first time in days, he permitted himself to think of her. Strange how after all this time, every meeting with her stood etched against the stormy background of their acquaintance. Most often in his thoughts, he saw her in that yellow and white dress, his unclaimed bride.

Wise in the ways of evil men, Gideon sewed his money into his clothing and kept out only enough to hire rude lodgings for the winter. He couldn't expose Dainty Bess to the freezing days and colder nights. Besides, until spring came and he could travel, it didn't matter where he stayed. Gideon settled down into his new world and became part of it.

For the first time, he patronized the gambling halls, never to bet heavily but enough to feel the deadly hold on men's hearts and souls. Was this how Cyrus had felt, urged on and radiant when winning, desperate when luck smiled on others and turned a cold shoulder on him? In an amazing streak of luck, Gideon won a sum large enough to send a gleam into the eyes of those at the table. Unwilling to become the target of men who thought nothing of killing for gold, he took advantage of an old trapper's offer to accompany him on his lines and get away from town. All winter, he remained with the mountain man but refused to go mining the next spring.

"You've been good to me," he told the bearded miner turned trapper. "Here, take this grubstake. Find yourself a mine."

"If I do, I'll find you and pay it back," the man promised. But Gideon laughed and rode away. The chances of striking it rich always loomed large in the men's minds.

He drifted north through Colorado and Wyoming, then into Montana. Spring, summer, and fall, he hired out on ranches, glad for the riding and roping. Yet in late fall, almost a year from his hasty wedding and departure from Texas, he faced himself in a bunkhouse mirror far from home and sighed. Money, he had. Comrades, as many as he would let be friends. Peace, there was none.

He scowled. *Was there no spot on earth where he could be at peace with the past?* Drifting hadn't been the answer, but neither had ignoring God. He remembered the kindliness of the trapper and the long, companionable tramps on the trap line. The next morning, he quit his job and rode south in search of another quiet winter like the year before. To his amazement, hordes of people had poured into the area.

"What's happening?" he demanded of a red-faced cowhand hitching his horse to a rail before a new saloon.

"Where yu been, Mister? Thought everyone knew about the boom." The amiable cowpoke grinned and told Gideon a miner had struck it rich nearby, bought half the town, and was "nee-go-she-ating" for the other half. "If yu want a job, his office is over there." The hand pointed to a new log building across the busy street.

Curious, Gideon ambled over and was met with a bear hug like he'd never had before. The strike-it-rich miner was the same man who had taken Gideon on his line and been grubstaked by the Texas rider. His gratitude knew no limits. He installed Gideon in the best room in the finest hotel that had sprung up and opened an account for him in the new bank that made the young man's eyes pop.

He also gave Gideon some advice. "Son, I don't know where you came from, but if you're as smart as you appear to be, you'll buy yourself a ranch somewhere, maybe Arizona. You've got enough money to stock it and hire good hands. Find yourself a pretty western gal, have some kids, be happy. Wish I'd done that."

Gideon's heart leaped at the idea of owning a ranch, but then his mind intruded. What good would it be without the wife and kids he could never have? A mocking little voice added what his heart could not, *What good without Judith?*

CHAPTER 11

The second winter Gideon spent in Colorado was nothing like the first. No longer a trapper's helper but a valued friend and guest in Tomkinsville, as the boom town was now called after its new owner, he spent his days playing cards in the saloon. He even picked up the coarse language of his fellow gamblers, drank for the first time in his life, and bitterly blamed God for his past. His one pleasure in his downward slide was that he now used his treacherous brother's name as his own. If anyone had told Tomkinsville that "Cyrus Scott" had once been a preacher, no one would have believed it. The few times he allowed himself to drink too much, he passionately hoped news of his tough reputation would get back to his father. If it did, Lige would admit fault in the son he had felt did no wrong.

Gideon also learned to fight and licked a half dozen cowhands known for their skill with fists. He carried his gun, remembering Lige's words that men would respect him once he'd proven himself.

Ironically, the situation Gideon had avoided like riding through a cactus patch prompted his first gunfight. A young woman named Lily, the newest of those who sang and danced in the saloon, caught his attention. Her dark eyes reminded him of Judith, and she didn't seem to belong. He befriended her, then encouraged her to leave and go elsewhere. If Lily stayed in this ungodly atmosphere, she wouldn't be able to hold out for long.

"I've got plenty of money to get you started," he told her simply. Some of the old goodness that life had erased from his face shone again. "Is Lily your real name?"

She shook her head, and red flags waved in her dusky skin.

"Good. Go to Denver or Colorado Springs or anywhere. How did you ever fall into this miserable life, anyway?"

"My parents died. I had to do something to live." Lily suddenly looked older than her seventeen years.

A pang went through Gideon. *Judith had been desperate, too, trying to earn a living for herself and Joel. What if she were forced into such work?*

Never! his mind shouted. He squared his shoulders. *Neither should this young woman.* He waited while she gave notice to the saloon owner, then escorted her to the first outgoing stage, warmed in spite of the snappy cold weather by her broken, "God bless you."

Gideon's action did not endear himself to the saloon keeper and his friends. A few days after Lily left, Sears, the biggest and meanest of them, drawled, "Too bad the rest of us ain't well heeled like Scott here. We coulda set Lily up right smart an' had us a cozy little —"

A well-placed blow cut off the suggestion. His eyes blazing, Gideon leaped from his chair at the card table and faced the foul-mouthed man. "It's men, no, *animals* like you that ruin women who have nowhere to go. You're a rotten lot!"

"An' you think *yore* better?" The humiliated Sears reached for his gun. Gideon's shot knocked it out of his hand before it ever cleared the holster.

"One more crack like that about any woman, and I'll kill you!" He backed from the saloon into black night, his gun held steady in case one of the others tried anything. Once outside, he dodged behind buildings, more afraid of himself and God than of being followed. What had he come to — Gideon Scott, whose bright and promising career had been cut off?

Revulsion filled him. His stomach heaved, and it took supreme control to keep from retching. Once he could have defended Lily by using God's Word. Now he looked down at the gun he still held. Cold sweat drenched him. Had his threat been valid? Would he have killed another human being?

Somehow he reached his hotel room and barred the door. When he lighted his lamp, the wild-eyed apparition he beheld brought his gun up until he realized he faced the mirror above the bureau.

"Who's there?" Gideon spun. The room lay silent, empty except for himself and his mirrored reflection. "Who spoke?" he demanded, wondering if he were going mad, trying to remember where he had heard those words and when.

"The prodigal son." Gideon dropped heavily onto the bed. "Luke 15. 'A certain man had two sons.'" Uncontrollable laughter shook him. "And all these years I thought the story reversed, that the elder son, Cyrus, was the prodigal!" The rest of the parable on which he had preached a half dozen sermons came back: The younger boy went to a far country, wasted his money in riotous living, and found himself in want, hungry and sick. " 'And when he came to himself, he said —' " Gideon choked. " 'Father, I have sinned against heaven.' Oh, dear God, what am I doing here?" Desolation greater than any he had known swept through him. Tonight he might have killed a man. If he kept on with the way he now lived, he couldn't avoid bloodshed. He had seen it in the eyes of the onlookers when he drew his gun with lightning speed. Every would-be gunslinger jealous of his reputation would be standing in line. Kill or be killed, the law of the frontier.

Yet unlike the repentant sinner in the parable, Gideon could not return to his earthly father. He could always return to his loving heavenly Father and find peace and a measure of comfort that might help to heal his shattered, lonely life. Before he slept, he had poured out his heart in prayer and slept as he hadn't slept since he left the Circle S. Tomorrow he would follow his benefactor's advice and ride out and find a ranch somewhere. Arizona appealed to him: plenty of land for those who were willing to work for it, defend themselves from Apaches, and dig in. Something of the range-loving boy he had been still lived inside Gideon. After a prayer of thanks to God for bringing him to himself, he slept and dreamed of a new, brighter day, one that might sometime lead to exoneration and Judith.

With a thundering knock and crashing of wood, armed, angry men stormed into his room later that night. Gideon bounded from bed, trying to make sense of the confusion. A match flared. Rude hands grabbed him. Oaths fell on his ears like hail. "Git yore pants on," he was ordered while someone lighted the lamp.

With a wrenching effort, he tore free. "I demand to know why you are here." Something in his face halted his attackers but not for long.

"Yu've got yore nerve. First you shoot up Sears in the saloon, then trail him to his shack an' knife him."

The low grumble sent horror into Gideon. He had heard of mobs who hanged accused persons first and asked questions later. "Fools," he cried. "I could have killed him when I shot him, you all know that. Why would I wait and take a chance of him getting me?" He saw uncertainty grow in some of the faces. "Do you think I'm that loco? Your friend outweighed me by at least forty pounds."

"What good is that when some jasper sticks a knife in your back?" someone called.

The crowd's mood turned ugly again with "Hang him" and "String him up" heard from all corners.

"That will be just about enough of that." The quiet but deadly voice from the doorway stopped the yelling. Tomkins stood cradling a sawed-off shotgun. He patted it significantly. "This gun here's touchy, boys. Used it to stand off claim jumpers, grizzly bears, all kinds of undesirable critters." He looked at Gideon. "What's all this uproar?"

"Sears and I had an argument. He drew on me, but I beat him and shot the gun out of his hand, then came home. I don't know anything more. These, er, gentlemen seem to think I sneaked up on him and knifed him."

"You didn't, did you?" Tomkins's eyes gleamed.

Gideon shook his head, but someone cried, "He lies!"

For a single heartbeat, Gideon once more stood defying his father. The same words he used with Lige fell from his lips in a hotel room hundreds of miles away. "I have never lied, and I never will to save my reputation or to save my life. I know nothing of who stabbed Sears." He tensed, ready to spring if Tomkins didn't believe him. When the big head nodded, Gideon relaxed.

"D'yu have a knife?" an unconvinced man bellowed.

"Of course. Every rider carries a knife."

"Look like this one?" The triumphant man held out a knife, careful to touch only the tip.

Gideon shuddered at the ghastly dark stains on the blade that glinted wickedly in the dimly lit room. "It's ordinary enough to look like mine."

"Where's yore knife?" the questioner demanded.

"In my saddlebag hung on the nail in the livery stable," Gideon told him.

"Who knows it's there?" Tomkins asked with a concerned expression on his lined face.

Gideon shrugged. "Anyone who may have looked in the saddlebags." Alarm triggered inside him.

"How come yu leave yore knife there?" the persistent voice went on.

Gideon put both hands on his hips and glared. "I've never used a knife except for range work. I didn't think I'd need it here in the hotel."

"Best we mosey on down to the stable and have a look-see." Tomkins stood aside to let the others pass, then ordered, "Stop! On second thought, I'll just make sure no one decides to tamper with evidence by removing Scott's knife just as a friendly little joke." His tone left no uncertainty as to the fate of a person who tried it.

Gideon pulled on his clothes and a heavy jacket, glad his bankbook lay carefully hidden inside the jacket lining. If the worst happened, perhaps he could leap to Dainty Bess's back and ride out.

Ten minutes later, Tomkins unwillingly ordered the sheriff to lock up Gideon until the case could be looked into more thoroughly. There had been no knife in the saddlebag, and Sears lay close to death. "If he doesn't make it, you're safer here than at the hotel," Tomkins told the despairing young man. He scratched his grizzled jaw. "Don't worry. We'll get to the bottom of this, but I wish to God you'd taken my advice and got out of this place before getting yourself into trouble."

"So do I," Gideon said soberly. For a moment, he felt tempted to confess who he really was, how he'd taken his brother's name and hours before realized the dead-end trail he'd been riding. Realizing it could do more harm than good, he said nothing.

Strange how many times he had felt the silence before a storm. When Tomkinsville settled down for the rest of the night, not a dog barked. Even the light snow that had fallen earlier in the day ceased. Yet Gideon felt the same eerie sensation that preceded Cyrus's flight and Judith's arrival. Would he have another night of life? Would Tomkins's power in the boomtown be enough to sway the mob if Sears died?

"Well, God, if this is my last time to tell You I'm sorry for everything, especially for not trusting You, so be it." Gideon flung himself on the miserable excuse for a bed and hoped San Scipio would never learn what had befallen the minister they once revered.

Anxious days and high hopes followed black nights and despair for Gideon. Sears began to mend, then suffered a relapse. For three days, Tomkinsville held its breath but not its invective against the coward who had knifed him. Finally, the big man turned toward life and in a couple of weeks regained enough of his strength to respond to questions. Yet he seemed strangely reluctant to talk.

"Don't know what's got into him," Tomkins admitted with a worried frown. "Says he plans to talk when it will do the most good, at the trial." He sent Gideon a keen glance. "I'll be glad when this is all over. If you're cleared, you better skedaddle out of here. This whole thing has left a bad taste with folks. Even if you're innocent, you won't be popular in these parts." He stretched his big body. "Leastways, he didn't die. The most you can be charged with is attempted murder, which is bad enough."

After Tomkins had gone, Gideon met the Lord in prayer. "Dear God, is there a reason behind all this?" He refused to let his friend bail him out. Uncomfortable as it was, the jail offered a certain security in case Sears took a turn for the worse again.

Lulled by a sunny day that promised an early spring but had blizzards lurking up its sleeve, the citizens of Tomkinsville turned out in droves for the trial. Before going to the saloon-turned-courtroom, used because it was the largest building in town, Gideon prayed. "God, I have no defense but the truth. I commit my life into Your hands." He stopped, remembering the shock in Tomkins's face when he handed him the precious bankbook wrapped in brown paper and addressed to *Mrs. G. Scott, c/o Circle S Ranch, San Scipio, Texas.* "If anything happens, mail it."

Tomkins peered at the address. Gideon could see questions trembling on his tongue, but his loyal friend merely pocketed the package. "I'll return it after the trial," he said brusquely.

Colorado justice, often swift even when it wasn't sure, dragged while the prosecutor reached into his bag of tricks to impress the inhabitants of Tomkinsville. He painted a picture of the accused man that would have done Satan himself proud. In awful, rolling tones, he built up a setting in which Gideon, angered by his failure to kill Sears in a fair fight, vindictively followed the other man like a wolf stalking its prey. If Gideon hadn't known better, he would have been swayed by the man's false but vivid reenactment of attempted murder.

Under oath, Gideon admitted his knife had disappeared and the one used on Sears looked like it. However, he maintained that his shot in the saloon had gone exactly where he aimed it. "Sir, I've never killed a man, and I didn't mean to kill Sears."

"Then why did you say, and I quote, 'One more crack like that about any woman, and I'll kill you!' " The prosecutor fairly oozed satisfaction.

"I was angry."

"So angry you followed Sears and tried to finish the job." The prosecutor turned to the judge with a deliberate gesture. "I rest my case."

Tomkins himself had elected to defend

Gideon. He grinned when he stated flatly, "I'm no lawyer, but I carry considerable weight around here." Now he leisurely stood and walked to where he could face Gideon yet not block the judge's view of his face. "How long have you known me?"

"About a year and a half."

"Tell the court under what circumstances we met."

Gideon couldn't follow the line of defense in Tomkins's thinking but obediently recited, "I came here a year ago last fall, did some gambling, and won some money. Thought I'd be better off away from town, so I went trapping with you for the winter."

"And you grubstaked me in the spring so I could go back to mining. Me, a trapper and miner who'd never had much more than the clothes on my back."

"Yes."

"Judge, this man is the real reason why Tomkinsville is booming. If he hadn't been good to a broken-down old miner, why, none of our prosperity would have come!" He waved an expansive hand. "I tried to find him and repay him after I struck it rich, but it wasn't 'til he drifted back down from Wyoming and Montana that I could locate him." He stepped closer to Gideon and clapped him on the shoulder. "Scott's no more capable of knifing anyone in the back than, than you are, Judge!"

"Prove it!" shouted the red-faced prosecutor.

"I call as my witness, Eb Sears."

Gideon gasped, as did the judge, the prosecutor, and every man present.

"Now, Mr. Sears, tell us in your own words what happened," Tomkins said, "and tell it straight."

Before he began, Sears shot an unreadable look at Gideon. "Aw, I was drunk and loud. Said some things about Lily I knew weren't true. He hit me. I got mad and drew. So did he." Sears pointed to Gideon, who silently prayed and clenched his hands into fists.

"In your opinion, did Mr. Scott try to kill you and miss, the way the prosecutor said?" Tomkins probed.

"Naw." A reluctant respect and a personal code Gideon wouldn't have expected from Sears straightened the slumping witness. "He's chain lightnin' and could shoot the eye out of a mosquito."

A little ripple of surprise ran through the room, and Gideon felt himself start to sweat. The next few moments could mean the difference between conviction and freedom.

"Mr. Sears, under oath, did Cyrus Scott knife you? You've been strangely silent ever since it happened."

Sears scratched his head. "At first, I thought so. Seemed logical. Then I started wonderin'. If he wanted to kill me, he shore coulda done it in the saloon, with everybody there havin' to testify I drew first. Naw, I don't think he knifed me."

"Do you have any idea who might have?"

Stone-cold, dead silence followed the question.

"Mr. Sears, I repeat, do you have any suspicions? Did anyone hate you enough to do this?"

Sears grunted. "I ain't the best-liked hombre in Tomkinsville." He hesitated, then said, "I've had a lot of time to think. Maybe it wasn't exactly me someone was after."

The ripple grew to a murmur, stilled when the judge banged his gavel on the bar. "Silence!"

"Just what do you mean?" Tomkins leaned forward. So did Gideon.

Sears squirmed. "I don't like accusin' anyone, but certain folks were real upset when Lily up and left."

"How do you know that?" Tomkins's voice cracked like a bullwhip.

"Lily told me." Red crawled into the

tanned face. "Said when she quit, the boss ranted and raved and said he'd get even with Scott." The red deepened, but Sears looked square at Tomkins. "Maybe he saw this as a good chance. Besides, we'd had a fallin' out over the girl. I was sweet on her, and so was he, and 'til Scott came, she sorta liked me. I'da married her." He hung his head and stared at the floor. "That's why when I said all that stuff about Lily I knew wasn't true, it was 'cause I was jealous." His head snapped back up. "I shouldn't have been. Lily told me flat out Scott never asked nothin' from her, which is more than some —"

"Liar!" The saloon owner stood and clawed for his gun. "Too bad you didn't die when I knifed you."

"Hold it right there." A gun had miraculously sprung to the visiting judge's hand. Tomkins and the sheriff disarmed the raving man, whose tongue had been loosed by too many drinks he had served to his friends and himself, celebrating Gideon's conviction prematurely.

"Best one I ever had here." His eyes blazed hatred for both Sears and Gideon. "Those innocent types bring in customers, but she'd have come around if it hadn't been for you." He spat in their direction.

"Can't tell me Scott doesn't have her waiting for him somewheres. Men don't help women like Lily unless there's something in it for them. I fixed him, stole his knife —"

The judge cut into the babbling. "Mr. Scott, you are cleared and free to go. Sheriff, lock up this murderer! He's confessed, and I sentence him to . . ."

Gideon missed the rest amid the wild cheer that shook the rafters. With Tomkins leading him, he walked out, feeling free and dirty. His sin had led to this moment, and he knew it would take a long time to rid himself of the taint of Tomkinsville.

Chapter 12

Just before Christmas of 1876, Gideon, who had now reverted to using his own name, reined in his horse and surveyed his earthly kingdom. After traveling through much of Arizona, thrilled by its deserts and plateaus, chastened by the expanse of blue sky that make the red-rock canyons and monuments even more torrid, he had found the Double J spread not far from Flagstaff. *The name holds a certain appeal,* he ruefully admitted.

He sobered when he considered what Judith and Joel would think of Double J, surrounded by oak and manzanita, sage and pine. There were cattle enough for a good start, thanks to Tomkins. One thing Gideon had done before leaving Colorado was to seek out those whose money he had won in gambling and repay them. He would not begin his rededicated life with the Lord by building on tainted money nor under a false name. Before he left Tomkinsville, he told the whole story to his benefactor.

"You love the lass, your wife?" Tomkins shot a keen glance into his eyes.

"More than life, second only to God."

"Son, things have a way of working out. Go on out to Arizona. Get settled. Be God-fearing, honest, and work hard." Wistfulness crept into his eyes. "If I were younger, I'd go with you." But Tomkins shook his shaggy head. "Maybe one day you'll see me come riding in if my luck breaks. I've got a lot salted away, but as long as I keep finding more, I suppose I'll stay here."

"You'll always be welcome." A hard grip of hands, and Gideon rode away knowing he'd always have a friend in the man he once so carelessly helped.

Now he sat easily in the saddle and wondered what came next. He'd been from Tucson to the Grand Canyon of the Colorado River, from the White Mountains to the Mogollon Rim and into the Tonto. Yet something about the Flagstaff area held him. He thought of the group of settlers who had camped there not long before. They made a flagstaff from a pine tree and flew the American flag from it. Folks said the incident provided the name for the birth of a town.

The knowledge of men Gideon had gained

both from preaching and wandering proved invaluable in selecting cowboys for the Double J. "Don't hire just anyone," Tomkins had warned. "Handpick wranglers who'll give you loyalty, not just a day's work."

Gideon heeded the advice. He never hired a hand who couldn't look him straight in the eye without wavering. He never hired a man who shifted when he spoke. He made it clear there would be no red-eye on the job, and if he heard of any man getting "likkered up" on Saturday night, that hand could pack his gear and ride out.

"Aw, Boss, what're you runnin', a Sunday school?" Gideon's foreman, Fred Aldrich, complained. "How'm I s'posed to keep a wild bunch of cowboys workin' if they can't bust loose on the weekends?"

"When you hire them, tell them what the rules are and remind them we may have a hot enough time if the Apaches hit us," Gideon told him.

Aldrich heaved a sigh clear from his dusty boot tips to the crown of the sweat-stained Stetson that shaded his keen, dark eyes. "We're gonna be the laughin' stock of all Arizony," he muttered, but faithfully carried out his orders. Because Gideon knew his standards would make it hard to get riders, he not only paid top wages but promised that any cowboy who stayed a year or more would get a bonus. The offer, a share in the Double J or a good horse and saddle, hit Arizona like a desert storm. Aldrich stuck his tongue in his cheek and solemnly confirmed the offer, sourly adding, "That's what comes of havin' a boss from Texas. Thinks his way's the only way, and shoot, he might just be right!"

Wide-shouldered, grinning cowboys, some still in their teens, came out of curiosity but stayed because of their new boss. They differed from the Texas cowboys in subtle ways. Arizona demanded more daring men because of its raw newness. It cared little for background, everything for the measure of a man. Gideon's outfit answered to names like Lonesome and Cheyenne, Kansas and Dusty. No one asked where the riders came from, and prying into a rider's past was taboo.

Gideon sometimes found this tolerance maddening, and he blew up to Aldrich one day. "Everyone knows that Stockton, who's planning to run cattle in the Tonto, is a notorious outlaw going respectable."

"Shore, Boss. Arizony's always willin' to give a man a second chance." He shrugged. "This territory's gonna be a state someday, and if it takes reformed crooks to do it, so what? Out here, long as a man's goin' straight, we figger more power to him." He half closed his eyes. "On the other hand, we also keeps our eyes peeled so he don't go back to his takin' ways, takin' other folks' property."

Gideon subsided. Who knew better than he the need for a second chance?

Although the Navajo had been put down, their final defeat coming in a fierce 1864 campaign led by the famed scout Kit Carson, the Apache had not. Small bands terrorized and raided. Cochise and Geronimo were names to respect. They led warriors against forts, towns, and lonely ranches, but the settlers were still determined to find homes. Hunted and forced farther back into the remote and seemingly impenetrable canyons, infuriated by broken treaties, the original Arizona inhabitants fought for their lives.

So far, the Double J hadn't been a target, but the threat was ever present. In some ways, Gideon pitied the Navajo and Apache. How would he feel if a horde of strangers came in and took his land? Even in the short time he had owned the Double J, he had grown to love it. With every sunrise, he looked east and thought of the past. Each sunset brought a feeling of well-being along with gloriously painted skies. He had finally conquered the poignant regret of his sins; if God had forgiven him, he had no right not to forgive himself. A desire to return to the Lord's service haunted him. Yet how could he?

That desire continued to grow. Now and then, he rode into Flagstaff on Sunday, wishing there were a church. His restlessness finally made Aldrich ask, "What's eatin' you, Boss? Yore jumpier than a fish swimmin' upstream."

Gideon took a deep breath. "Fred, what would the boys say if I invited folks out from town, anyone who cared to come, for Christmas? We could decorate and have candy for the kids and read the Christmas story out of the Bible. Sing songs, too."

Aldrich considered. "Might not be a bad idea. I reckon the boys could stand such goin's-on for once." He cocked his head to one side. " 'Tain't none of my business, but who're you aimin' on havin' read that story?"

"I thought I would," Gideon told him frankly. He looked around the large room. "Think it will hold everyone?"

"All those who'll come," Fred said cryptically. "The boys and me can stay in the kitchen if this room fills up." He grinned.

"It'll be pure pleasure for us to do yore decoratin' after all the hard work we've put in this fall. By the way, Boss, now that winter's comin', what about the hands? Are you layin' them off like most of the other ranchers do?"

"Nope. Every day that's nice enough, we'll be busy working. I want this ranch house expanded. We'll add a second story —"

"Whoopee!" Aldrich's face split wide open, and he howled like a banshee. "You must be aimin' to get hitched, huh, Boss?"

Gideon's excitement died. "No."

Red faced, Aldrich broke off his rejoicing. "Sorry, Boss." He hastily stood and mumbled, "I better go see what the boys are up to. Anyhow, they'll be glad to hear they won't be loafin' this winter." He backed out, obviously embarrassed.

Gideon realized the crisp air straight off the San Francisco mountains had worked through his heavy jacket. Late December was no time to dream outdoors. The boys would be waiting for him to give instructions about decorating. They'd ridden out and gathered pungent boughs, laughing and predicting how many would come out from town for "the boss's Christmas." Gideon had overheard Lonesome say, "Bet he's doin' this so we-all won't get to drinkin'.

I'd sure like to wet my whistle, but I got my eye on a purty little gal in town. If I stick it out and get to be part owner of this here ranch, she's bound to see what a steady feller I am and slip into harness with me."

A roar of laughter followed Lonesome's confidence, but Gideon knew it was good-natured. The boys wouldn't admit it for a gold mine, but Aldrich had let it slip how proud they were to "help make Christmas for folks, 'specially the little ones."

"Tell them to wear their best," Gideon said. "This is their celebration, too."

Before bedtime on Christmas Eve, the ranch house smelled of fresh greens. Rude benches had been nailed together and lined the walls to give seating space. Gideon's original plan to have a service and treats for the children had met with frowning disapproval from his outfit. Aldrich reminded him, "Folks're comin' from miles around, the way I hear it."

The boys nodded solemnly, and Aldrich went on. "Seems downright unneighborly not to give 'em dinner."

"*Dinner!* Can we handle it?"

"Hey, Boss, when're you gonna get on to Arizona?" asked Lonesome, always the most talkative of the cowboys. "Just put the word out we'll all be havin' Christmas dinner here, and folks'll be cookin' for days ahead. Wimmenfolk like to shine, and what better place than makin' food for us pore, unfortunate cowboys?"

Gideon sensed a new camaraderie with his men. In a reckless but appreciative mood, he laughed and held up his hands in mock defeat. "All right, but be it on your heads. You'll have to help, and everyone who sticks and helps make this the best Christmas these settlers have seen in many a day gets a ten-dollar Christmas present."

"Yippee!" they chorused, but Lonesome had to have the final word. "I think I just died and went to heav'n, boys. I thought I heard the boss say ten dollars."

"Aw, you've chased so many critters and listened to them beller yore ears are as bad as yore eyesight," Aldrich told him, but the approval in his foreman's dark eyes told Gideon how far he had come with his hands.

Shortly after breakfast on Christmas Day, by buckboard and wagon, on fine horses and half-wild mustangs, the invited guests began coming. Every family brought enough food for a cavalry! Gideon started, dismayed. *What did he know about serving such a bounteous dinner?* As if reading his mind, the women shooed him out of his own kitchen and told him to go "visit the menfolk" and leave them to their work. Although he had thought his bunkhouse cook more than adequate, he revised his opinion when he saw the groaning table laden with Arizona and holiday specialties.

A billowy matron who had taken charge ordered everyone inside, shushed them, and made an announcement to Gideon. "Mr. Scott, this dinner's in honor of the Almighty's Son. It's proper and fittin' for us to give thanks." Without a pause, she bowed her head and prayed, "Lord, on this special day we give thanks for food and friends and Your goodness to us. Amen."

Gideon silently thanked God she hadn't asked him to pray. He found himself suddenly speechless at his overwhelming love for these people, longing for home and thankful. Two Christmases ago, when he had been out on the trapline with Tomkins, they'd celebrated by cooking an extra portion of rice and dried fruit to go with their venison. Last year, to his shame, he had spent Christmas gambling his life away in the saloon at Tomkinsville. His heart felt as though it were bursting. *God, thank You that at least I'm not there.*

When everyone finished eating and even the cowhands admitted that after four or five helpings, things didn't taste so good anymore, the women packed everything away. Round-eyed children sat on blankets on the floor, and Gideon knew the time had come for his "service." He refused to remember other services, the real ones when he openly preached. To do so would leave him unable to continue.

He faced his guests, noting how lone riders who had "dropped by" rubbed elbows with settlers, how former outlaws chatted with the children. In the spirit of Christmas, disagreements and differing viewpoints faded. Gideon smiled. "It's been an honor for my outfit and me to have you come." He saw the boys swell with pride. "We have a little treat for the children, but first, as has been said, it's fitting for us to recognize whose birthday this is. I thought we could sing some carols."

Never had he heard the enthusiasm with which these brave pioneers sang. "Joy to the World" literally shook the ranch house as did "Hark, the Herald Angels Sing" and "O Come, All Ye Faithful." Voices lowered on "Silent Night," and Gideon saw eyelashes blink to hide wavering emotions. When the last note died, Gideon took out his Bible. "I'd like to read from the second chapter of Luke." He steadied his voice.

" 'And it came to pass in those days, that

there went out a decree from Caesar Augustus, that all the world should be taxed. . . .' "
On and on went the story, unfolding with new meaning as it had for so many years. Gideon read straight through the angels' proclamation to the shepherds, " 'Glory to God in the highest, and on earth peace, good will toward men.' " The shepherds then rose and went to Bethlehem and found Mary and Joseph and the baby Jesus, not in the fine inn, but quartered in humble surroundings such as these Arizona settlers knew so well. " 'And the shepherds returned, glorifying and praising God for all the things that they had heard and seen, as it was told unto them,' " he quoted in closing.

A power greater than his own prompted him to add, "Shall we pray?" He bowed his head, and lamplight shone on his golden hair, for the winter day had been short. "Father, may we, too, glorify and praise You for all these things. In Jesus' name. Amen."

Gideon raised his head. He saw the astonishment in the faces of Aldrich, Lonesome, and many others. *What should he say?*

"Mama, is it time for the treat?" A patient child in her mother's arms broke the silence, and the crowd laughed while memories of the Christmas service retreated to the shadowy corners but remained a vivid part of the day.

"It truly is!" Gideon picked up the little girl and set her on his shoulder the way he used to do with Joel. A pang went through him, but he smiled and went to the carefully prepared little papers of candies he and the boys had painstakingly counted out and wrapped. "Merry Christmas, Honey. Come on, all you buckaroos. There's enough for everyone!" A swarm of eager but well-mannered children surrounded him. "Here, Fred, boys, help me," he called.

Five minutes later, every child had found a spot on the floor to enjoy their candy and listen to the grown-ups talk about what a wonderful day it had been. But before the gathering dispersed for home, a little group of men and women approached Gideon. "Mr. Scott, you did fine with the reading and singing and all. The praying, too. Until we can get a church and a regular preacher, would you ride into Flag on Sunday afternoons and hold meetings? Our children need to be raised by the Book, and land sakes, none of us has time during the week."

He didn't hesitate an instant. "I would be proud if you really want me." Yet to accept their genuine offer without a confession would be hypocrisy. He clenched his hands behind his back and added, "There's something you must know first. I left Texas under a black cloud, accused of something I didn't do, but I couldn't prove myself innocent."

The woman who had offered the blessing smiled until her eyes disappeared into rolls of flesh. "If the truth were to be told — which it won't and don't need to be — other folks here are ridin' under some black clouds of their own, and they may not be so innocent, either!"

The crowd laughed, and the spokesman for the impromptu committee pressed, "This is a new land, and what's gone before is gone forever. Will you hold meetings?"

"I will." Gideon straightened to full height. "And I hope every one of you will come." In a wave of laughter and anticipation, the party broke up. The boys lingered in the ranch house as if reluctant to have the day end. Gideon watched their awkward attempts at busying themselves, taking out the crude table and benches, straightening sagging boughs. Finally he said, "Before it's chore time, I want to thank you all." He took a small stack of packages wrapped and tied with string in lieu of ribbon and began to distribute them. "Merry Christmas, boys."

"Aw, Boss, the ten dollars was enough,"

interjected Lonesome. "Why'd you go and buy us these, anyway?" He spread out warm, lined gloves, his face shining. "I never had no gloves as good as these."

A murmur of assent rose.

To break the emotion he felt crowding him, a straight-faced Gideon told them, "You'll need them when we start building on to the ranch house!"

The outfit groaned, but Aldrich stepped forward. He carried a bulky package. "This is for you, Boss."

Gideon felt like the little girl who had received the first packet of candy. He silently untied the package that Aldrich had set on the floor.

A saddle that must have cost every ranch hand a good share of a month's wages — the saddle every rider covets and seldom owns — glistened in front of him, its silver trim beckoning his touch.

Did good old Lonesome sense Gideon's confusion? "If we'da known a present would cut off yore speech, Boss, why, we'da given it to you a couple of weeks ago when you gave Aldrich orders for us to dig holes for fenceposts!"

They trooped out, devilment clear in their lean faces, leaving Gideon only enough time to call, "Thanks," and weakly sink into a chair, then stare at Aldrich. When the door closed behind the last of the boys, he asked, "Was the saddle your idea?"

"Naw." Aldrich shook his head, and enjoyment of the situation showed plain in his eyes. "Lonesome brought it up, and the rest of the boys wished they had." His grin matched the mischief in the younger hands' faces when he added, "Glad it caught you by surprise. It woulda ruinated everythin' if you'd made some stupid remark about it bein' too much." A warning lay beneath his casual words. He headed for the door and paused with one hand on the knob. Gideon could feel something coming and tensed.

"Folks around here will respect yore mentionin' about Texas and why you left," Aldrich drawled. "Once it's been said, though, no need to talk anymore." He lifted one eyebrow and grinned again. "Merry Christmas, Boss."

"Merry Christmas." Gideon watched his foreman turn up his coat collar against the cold night air before stepping out. The latch clicked, and boot heels thudded across the porch. The silence that follows the emptying of a house when Christmas is over fell, leaving Gideon to wonder, *Surely this silence couldn't herald the coming of another storm.* He had confessed the worst, and these new neighbors cared little.

Yet within an hour, the snow came, enshrouding the Double J and obliterating all trace of the merrymakers who had come, eaten, and worshiped together, then gone back to their own homes, leaving Gideon with his memories.

CHAPTER 13

Spring in all its glory came to Arizona. Trees greened, budded, and burst into new life, and so did Gideon. The long winter months hadn't been idle, yet he had found time to regain his perspective. He returned to studying his Bible and, when weather permitted, rode or drove into Flagstaff to hold simple Sunday afternoon services composed of hymns, a Scripture reading, and sometimes a short lesson. Gideon always returned home more blessed than his informal congregation. If at times he longed to preach, he restrained himself. Although his bitterness against God had long since fled, he knew the time wasn't right. In the meantime, Aldrich and at least some of the boys usually came to the meetings, often slipping into the last of the benches set up in a cleaned-out barn.

"The Lord began His ministry in a stable. I reckon we can be glad to have a dry place for our meetings," folks said. They bundled in layers upon layers of clothes for the short services and grimly proclaimed that before snow flew the next fall, there'd be a regular church. The stove the barn owner generously put in kept only those in the first few rows warm.

Often while watching the snow fall, listening for the sound of laughter from the bunkhouse, Gideon felt the same uneasiness from the winter silence he'd experienced on Christmas Day. Yet as time passed, the feelings dwindled. The only unusual incident came when two of his outfit slipped the reins and came home from town bright eyed, talky, and smelling of drink.

"You know the rules, boys." Gideon faced his men, heartsick. "I won't stand for drinking."

The cowboys looked at each other, then with mutual appeal at Aldrich. The foreman shook his head, although Gideon saw how much he wanted to speak.

Lonesome took a deep breath. "Boss, we all know the rules, and these two mis'r'ble skunks don't deserve it. But yore always talkin' about how that Jesus feller in the Bible gave folks another chance if they were sorry." His keen eyes challenged Gideon. "Well, it doesn't take much to see how sorry lookin' they are." He pointed to the offenders, who sat on their bunks with heads drooping. Disarranged clothing spoke clearly that their pardners had already administered a certain amount of justice.

Lonesome went on. "We just don't want to have the Double J crew broke up." The memory of shared word and loyalty shone in his eyes and in the eyes of the others.

Gideon had the feeling he was on trial more than his men. With a quick prayer for guidance, he said, "All right. I'll let it go this one time but *never again.* If any of you ever come home drinking, pack and get your time. As for you —" He marched over to the culprits. "The offer's still good about earning a bonus, but you'll have to start your year as of right now, because I'm firing you and rehiring you this minute. Like it or lump it, and don't make me regret it."

"Fair enough." One of the cowboys held out his hand. Remorse for letting down the outfit and gladness for a second chance showed in his mighty grip. The second did the same. There might be grumbling later, but for now a sigh of relief swept through the bunkhouse, and Gideon went out feeling God had lent him for one night the wisdom of Solomon.

The threatened breakup of the Double J

217

wove unbreakable strands that held through temptation. With an outfit so determined to stay together, any cowpoke who even thought of straying found himself promptly rounded up and brought back to the straight and narrow. No one ever mentioned the boss's handling of the winter crisis, but the long hours of spring work and the spirits of his hands told Gideon the whole story.

Spring also brought problems. Aldrich dragged in long faced and angry one sunny afternoon. "Boss, our cattle are disappearin'."

"*Disappearing!* How?"

"Well, it ain't four-footed critters that are responsible," the foreman said sourly. "We found signs they're bein' driven. Rustled. Plumb stole right off the Double J."

"Indians?" A chill went up Gideon's spine.

Aldrich made a rude noise. "Naw. They kill a beef, take what they want, and let the rest lay." His eyes half closed in the way they did when he considered. "How about givin' me a few of the boys to scout out Stockton's place?"

"Take anyone you need. I'll be ready as soon as you are." Gideon jumped up and reached for his hat.

"You stay here, Boss. Me and Lonesome, Dusty, and Kansas can do the job. I'd take

Cheyenne, too, but he's sorer than a mule sittin' on a cactus. Toothache."

"I wouldn't think of letting you go without me," Gideon said blandly and caught the gleam in Aldrich's eyes, although he grumbled all the way out the door. Ten minutes later, the little band had mounted and headed toward Stockton's spread.

"I thought you were sick," Gideon told Cheyenne, whose swollen jaw gave mute evidence of pain.

"Not sick enough to miss the fun." He grinned crookedly. "I'm hankerin' to see what that bunch of yahoos does when we ride in."

"Who's *ridin'* in?" Aldrich demanded. His brows drew together over keen eyes. "We're scoutin', remember?"

"Yeah," Cheyenne hastily agreed, but not before Gideon saw the exchange of glances between the cowboys.

"No gunplay," he ordered, remembering the Tomkinsville saloon.

Lonesome, who could look cherubic in feigned indignation, retorted, "Why, Boss, are you loco? Us pore old cowpokes can't hardly bear to kill a rattlesnake." His remark dropped into a silence broken only by the rhythmic beat of their horses' hooves.

"I thought Stockton was supposed to be

reformed," Gideon mused aloud when they reached the borders of the former outlaw's ranch. "Why do you suspect him?"

"Suspect? We're just curious. Well, what d'you know!" Lonesome spurred his horse, and the others followed. "Funny, I'd swear that's a Double J brand on that steer." He pointed to a small bunch of cattle in a thrown-together corral. "There's another one. Mighty pee-coo-liar how they got in there, huh, Boss?"

Rage at the blatant thievery straightened Gideon's spine. His hot Texas blood boiled. "Stay here!" he ordered. Before his men could protest, he put Dainty Bess into a dead run toward the corral. Three men, none of them Stockton, leaped from their horses and faced him.

"What are you doing with my cattle in there?" Gideon yelled and pulled Bess up in front of them.

The sheer daring of his confrontation paralyzed Stockton's men. "Uh, they must have got mixed in when we brought in —"

"Liar!" Gideon bounded from the saddle. "Does Stockton know about this?" His voice rang in the clear air, and he read the answer in the men's faces. In a flash, Gideon leaped back onto Bess and uncoiled his lariat. Circling it over his head, he snugged it over

a poorly set fencepost. "All right, Bess!" *Crash!* The post gave way and dragged behind them. A mixture of Double J stock and other brands poured out to freedom.

"Yippee-i-ay!" Lonesome bellowed, then panic clutched his voice. "Boss, *look out!*"

His warning came seconds too late. Something struck Gideon squarely in the back. He reeled in the saddle, then fell to the ground, conscious of a volley of gunfire before the world went black.

As Judith Butler Scott in her yellow and white dress watched Gideon ride away from their wedding, something deep inside her begged him not to go. The truth she had begun to accept burst into full bloom: Gideon could not be guilty of the accusations she had made. His kisses confirmed it. Shy and reverent, they lingered on her lips and witnessed to his innocence. Blood pounded in her head. She rested her hands on Joel's shoulders for support. Would she ever see him again, this splendid man who had married her and ridden away for the sake of his family?

Somehow she pulled herself together. For Joel's sake, she must go on. Judith glanced at Lige Scott and shrank back from the naked heartbreak quickly veiled in his eyes.

His two sons were both gone. He turned and looked at Joel, and Judith shivered. She must fight, or Lige would take possession of the child in an attempt to create a second Cyrus. Despair filled her and blotted out everything but the need to walk carefully, at least for a time. Yet her heart cried out for help, and the peace of God strengthened her. She could do nothing until she regained her stamina lost through sickness and worry.

The journey to El Paso had seemed endless. The journey back felt even longer. Judith had the sensation of being smothered, imprisoned. Would the Circle S swallow her and Joel?

Naomi stirred beside her, smiled, and patted Judith's hand. Her low assurance, "Things won't seem so bewildering when we get home," did much to comfort the distraught bride. As long as Naomi remained her friend, Judith could survive.

To her surprise, once they reached the ranch, Lige helped her down and said gruffly, "You're our daughter now. Naomi will see you have what you need."

His rude attempt at kindness threatened the shaky control Judith struggled to maintain. "Thank you." She blinked hard. "Come, Joel." Tired from the long journey and excitement, he trotted after her, and after a hasty wash, they both fell asleep. They didn't waken until Carmelita tapped on their door and announced supper would be ready soon.

Although for a time Judith remained on guard, as early winter came, then blizzards beyond anything she and Joel had imagined, she learned to relax. She often felt as if they'd been on the Circle S forever. Lige gave an expurgated version of Gideon's absence, merely stating he had gone away for a time. Whether he believed Gideon would return was a matter between Lige and his God. He continued to treat Judith as the daughter he had called her and frankly idolized Joel. She worried, yet perhaps someday she could . . . Every time she got that far, she put it out of her mind. Her somedays were in God's hands.

The first spring after Gideon rode away brought Joel's fifth birthday and a beautiful collie pup from his grandfather. He promptly named it Millie after asking Judith, "Would Mama like it?"

"I'm sure she would." Judith hugged him to keep her tears from showing. Yet Joel owned a more priceless possession than earthly parents. His Friend Jesus was real to the boy, an ever-present comrade of the trail. Judith often marveled at the depth of his faith and prayed it would never be tarnished.

Summer, fall, winter, and a second spring elapsed, and nothing had been heard of either Gideon or Cyrus. New patches of white marred Lige's hair. A shadow lurked in Naomi's eyes even when she smiled and played with Joel, who adored her. Because of the distance to town, Naomi and Judith continued the child's education. Lige's sad eyes brightened when he saw how quickly Joel grasped the things he learned and put them into practice. He sent away for books to fill a library, and Joel discovered new worlds beyond the borders of Texas. Best of all, he loved the Bible stories Judith read to him.

A new minister had been installed in the San Scipio church, an older man with a kindly face and a great love of the Lord. He could not preach as Gideon had, but he taught the Word of God and people liked him. Only Lucinda Curtis openly mourned "the untimely and unexplained departure of Brother Scott."

Judith never knew how Lige managed it, but her marriage to Gideon remained unknown to San Scipio. Possessed of great power because of his large holdings, he didn't hesitate to wield it in his own interests. In any event, she gladly accepted the secrecy. Most of the fold in San Scipio would have exclaimed for a day or two, then continued to welcome her, except for Lucinda. Judith dreaded the other woman's bold attempts at companionship and pleaded Joel as an excuse to avoid the elaborate affairs given by Lucinda and her mother. Something in the washed-out gray eyes warned of a serpent's venom.

Joel's uncanny resemblance to the Scotts fed the gossip mill for a time until a drunken cowboy shot up San Scipio and turned attention toward himself. For the most part, Judith existed in a state of waiting, happy when she forgot she was Mrs. Scott, restless at other times.

Joel's growth and joy in everyone and everything on the Circle S helped her develop patience. She couldn't say what it was she waited for. Yet, how often in the evening her gaze turned west! Was Gideon somewhere beyond the horizon, struggling to patch up his life as best he could? Did he remember the woman he had married and renounced? If bright dewdrops sparkled in her lashes, no one knew but God. The love she held for her absent husband secretly warmed her. If they never met again in this life, they would in the next. She believed it with all her heart.

The summer of 1876 brought startling news to the Circle S in the form of a visitor. Tired, dusty, and determined, a big man rode in one early evening and asked to see Mrs. Scott. Rosa led him to the large room where the family gathered evenings before going to bed. The visitor looked around, noted each person present, and then strode directly toward Judith. "Mrs. Scott?"

"I am Mrs. Scott." Naomi stood, dignity in every line of her body.

"And you?" Keen eyes pierced Judith's confusion.

"I am Mrs. Gideon Scott."

"Ahh." A sigh of satisfaction lit the worn face.

"Who are you, and what do you want?" Lige put Joel off his knee and approached the man.

"I have news of your son. When have you heard from him?" The stranger's gaze bored into Lige, then turned back to Judith, ignoring Lige's strangled cry. Suddenly a great hand on his shoulder whipped him around, and Lige demanded, "What is your business here?"

"May I sit down? I've come a long way." The man didn't wait for permission but brushed dust from his pants and seated himself. "You have two sons, Cyrus and Gideon." He looked as if he were enjoying himself.

"Who are you?" Lige towered over him, but his hands shook.

"Tomkins is the name. In early winter of '74, I was running a trapline in Colorado. I'm a miner, but I was down on my luck and needed money for grub. A young feller rode in, took to gambling, and made a pile of money. He was smart enough to know it didn't make him popular, so he joined me trapping for the winter. In the spring, he grubstaked me."

"What was his name?" Lige's hands formed claws.

Judith held her breath, but let it out in a disappointed sigh when Tomkins spoke. "He called himself Cyrus Scott."

"Called himself! Wasn't that his name?" The great light of joy and hope dimmed in Lige's face.

"Turned out it wasn't. Anyway, he rode north. Said he aimed to work in Wyoming, maybe Montana." Tomkins grinned and rubbed his unshaven chin. "That summer I struck it big. Can't tell you how grateful I was to the young feller. Tried to find him and couldn't. Then just before snow flew, he came back to Tomkinsville, the boom-town that sprang up after the strike."

"Did you find out who he was?" Lige said hoarsely.

"Not then. I set him up in a hotel, put enough in the bank for him to buy a ranch, and told him to leave town." A dark cloud blackened Tomkins's face. "He hung around, though, befriended a saloon girl, nothin' more," he added when a little moan escaped Naomi's white lips. "Felt sorry for her, Ma'am. She was just a kid, so he gave her money to go away. Well, one of the bullies got likkered up, said some nasty things, and drew on my friend. Scott yanked out his gun quicker than lightning and shot the gun out of the scoundrel's hand."

He quickly sketched in the cowardly knife attack, the lynch mob, and the trial while his listeners sat wide-eyed and tense.

"Once cleared, Scott came to me and told me his story." Tomkins's gaze raked Lige. "How he got accused of something he didn't do on account of his brother."

"Gideon!" Judith's glad cry brought a smile to the leathery face.

"He rode out on the prettiest little sorrel mare I ever saw. Said he thought he'd take my advice and buy a ranch in Arizona. Oh, he gave back all the money he got gambling.

Tomkinsville's still talking about it." He scratched his head. "Didn't need it, anyway. He helped me, and I saw to it he had enough for that ranch and to get it stocked. I had business down this way and thought I'd stop by. Gideon's a proud man, and he never once lied. You might keep that in mind if you're still judging him." Tomkins got up, and in spite of the Scotts' offer of hospitality, he said he'd better mosey on. He walked out, spurs clinking.

Judith roused from the shock of all she'd learned and ran after him for a private word. "Mr. Tomkins, do you know where in Arizona my husband, er, Gideon might be?"

"No, Ma'am." He shook his head. "If I did, I'd be tempted to hunt him up. Fact is, I've been considering it ever since I left Colorado. Once I get done with my business, I might just head west instead of back home."

"Take me with you," she cried.

"You love him, Lass?"

"With all my heart, more than anything except God."

"Then it's all right." Tomkins smiled at her. "When I asked him that question, he said the same thing. 'More than life, second only to God.' I told him things had a way of working out."

"Bless you!" Judith impulsively stretched and kissed the grizzled cheek. "Will you take me to find him?"

"I reckon." Dull red suffused his face, but doubt crept into his eyes. "It might be better for us to wait and see if we can smoke out where he is. Can you be patient awhile longer, Lass?"

Torn between wanting to leave immediately and the common sense of his suggestion, she reluctantly nodded.

Tomkins promised, "I'll get my transacting done, see what I can learn, and stop back in a few weeks. A big company in Houston's been pestering me to sell out my holdings. I'm considering letting them have the whole shebang. I haven't had half the fun spending my gold as I did looking for it." His eyes twinkled. "Maybe I'll retire in Arizona and see if I can find a likely partner who'll sell me half ownership in a ranch."

"Don't say anything to the Scotts," Judith warned, hating herself but knowing it had to be said. "Lige won't let Joel go easily, especially when Gideon's involved." She proudly raised her head. "I won't sneak out when the time comes, but until it does, we have to live here."

Tomkins nodded. A few minutes later, he rode away, carrying Judith's hopes and dreams in his calloused hands. When Lige threw her a questioning look as she entered the big room, she simply said, "Gideon sends his love." Blushing, she fled before he had time to respond.

Judith expected to hear from Tomkins soon. Each time Lige picked up mail in town, she anticipated a letter. None came until just before Christmas. Tomkins had fallen ill in Houston and hadn't been able to do anything about locating Gideon. He then had to hurry back to Colorado to close a deal and get the mines sold. Now winter must pass before he could do more. He regretted it but was sending out letters to different parts of Arizona where Gideon might be. He promised that even if they came to naught, he'd come and get Judith in the spring. They'd follow the sagebrush trail and find her husband if it meant visiting every ranch in Arizona!

Resigned but impatient, again Judith settled down to wait.

CHAPTER 14

The shooting of Gideon was followed by a
burst of gunfire from the enraged Double J
riders that crippled two of the rustlers and
sent the third fleeing for his life. Enraged by
the incident, the worthy citizens of Flagstaff,
led by Aldrich, rose in mighty protest,
stormed in a body to Stockton, and tersely
told him to move on. "We can't prove for
certain yore in on it," the foreman snapped,
"but with our boss lyin' gunshot and the
doc sayin' he ain't sure if he can pull him
through, the Double J boys are a mite edgy."

Stockton's face showed his guilt, but he
sneered and told the volunteer posse, "I've
been planning to go, anyway."

"You'll stay healthier," Aldrich agreed. His
fingers crept suggestively to his pistol butt.
"I hear other parts of Arizony are more con-
doo-sive to a long life and better for rattle-
snakes."

A week later, Stockton vanished with his

herd, after a few interesting riders and Aldrich, in his words, "just moseyed by to make sure none of the Double J stock took it into their heads and follered."

Gideon lay bandaged and broken. The doctor who had been summoned from Phoenix shook his head when he saw the location of the bullet. Rolling up his sleeves, he promptly called for cauldrons of boiling water and set to work. Aldrich, in a brave effort to do anything to help, followed the doctor's barked commands as if he'd studied surgery for years. When the bullet had been extracted from its dangerously close position to Gideon's spine, the foreman stumbled from the room into the waiting group of cowboys.

"Well?" Lonesome's question and haggard face bore witness to the outfit's love for the boss.

Aldrich wiped great beads of sweat from his forehead. "How the deuce do I know? Doc says he won't be able to tell for at least twenty-four hours, if then."

"How bad is it?" Dusty demanded, his face dark.

"If it had been a half inch closer to his spine, he'd have never walked again. As it is . . ." The foreman shrugged and mopped his face again.

"We should've killed them galoots outright!" Cheyenne stared at his friends.

"Naw, the boss hates killin'," Lonesome reminded. He turned back to Aldrich. "Anythin' we can do?"

"Just pray." Silence fell on the motley group, broken only when someone coughed and another shuffled a worn boot. One by one, the hands slipped out. If they followed the foreman's advice, only they and "the boss's God" would know.

For a week, Gideon's life hung in the balance. The Phoenix doctor stayed on, enlisting the help of Aldrich or one of the boys to watch while he snatched fragments of sleep. Gideon mumbled, cried out, and whispered, but loyal punchers who sat for hours by his bedside and gave him sips of water kept their mouths shut. Not even with one another would they discuss what they heard. More than once, whoever rode herd on Gideon came out of his room with a thoughtful expression on his face. The relationship between the boss and God became clearer than ever during his delirious state.

"If he dies, I'm goin' after Stockton," Lonesome told Aldrich.

The old warhorse of a foreman, aged by years of worry and danger, shook his head. "Gideon wouldn't want that." If Lonesome noticed the change of address from *the boss* to *Gideon,* he didn't let on. Instead, he reluctantly admitted, "Yeah, too bad."

Slowly the dreaded fever cooled. On the eighth day, Gideon opened his eyes, unsure of where he was. Aldrich stood bent over him. "Don't try and talk. Yore better, and I'll get the doc."

Reassured, the injured man relaxed and slept. The second time he woke, his stomach felt hollow as a log and the dizziness in his head had settled down. But not until days later, when Aldrich and Lonesome got him up and he took a few shaky steps, did he see any of them grin.

"Whoopee!" The outfit yelped and beat their hats against their jeans. "Can't keep our Texas boss down." Leaning heavily on his supporters, Gideon dropped into a chair with obvious relief, an effort almost ignored by his friends.

"Vamoose, cowpokes, and let him rest," Aldrich ordered, and the laughing bunch roared outside to let off all the steam they'd stored up during Gideon's danger.

"Your face is blacker than a midnight storm," Gideon accused his foreman. "What's eating you?"

Aldrich slowly sat down opposite him and fiddled with his hat. "I've got a kinda confession to make."

Gideon stretched and winced when the still-healing muscles pulled. How good it felt to be alive and able to walk! "Shoot."

"The night the doc said he didn't know if you'd pull through, he said we oughta notify yore next of kin. I snooped around and put some of yore mumblings together and —"

Gideon froze. "You did *what?*"

Aldrich's plaintive tone told how much he hated his confession. "I wrote to yore — to Mrs. Judith Scott at San Scipio, and told her you were lyin' here shot up."

Every nerve in Gideon's body tingled. He stared, open-mouthed, unsure whether to whoop with joy or bawl out Aldrich for interfering in what didn't concern him.

The foreman stood and regained his usual cool manner. "Just thought I'd mention it in case, uh, we get unexpected vis'tors." He clinked out before Gideon could speak.

Visitors! What if Judith and Joel should one day walk through the door of his Arizona ranch house? For the first time, he admitted the building he and his men had done that winter represented the dream they would come. He lost himself in reverie for a time, then sternly put his memories aside. Nothing had changed, except he'd gotten himself shot up, and the doc said he might never ride straight again and might walk with a limp. "Lucky at that," Doc added sourly, but Gideon just smiled. He knew the doc pretty well now, and the dedicated man would be the first to give credit to the Great Physician who pulled Gideon back from death.

He wished Aldrich hadn't told him about the letter as weeks passed and no answer came. His final hope of someday clearing himself and returning home at least for a visit flickered and went out. "Well, God, it's just us again. I'll do the best I can and trust You," he said one dusky evening when the sun's passing left trails of red and purple in the western sky. Yet he wistfully turned east and added, "But please, be with the boy — and her — and make them happy."

Hundreds of miles east of the Double J, life on the Circle S splintered with the arrival of a scrawled note. Unsigned and dirty, as if carried and passed hand to hand for weeks, the smudged name ELIJAH SCOTT with the address following was almost illegible. "What's this?" Lige demanded when Carmelita brought it to him at the supper table in early spring. He opened it, stared, and jerked as if shot. "Carmelita, where did this come from?"

Her liquid brown eyes held no guile as she said, "A man threw it from a horse and rode away, even though I called, 'Señor, do you not want to water your horse?' "

With a loud cry, Lige pushed his chair back from the table with such a mighty thrust, it overturned and crashed to the floor. He rushed to the door, yanked it open, and disappeared, leaving the door swinging. Naomi, Judith, Carmelita, and a wide-eyed Joel stared after him, then Judith came to her senses. Vaguely aware of boots pounding toward the corral, she snatched the grimy missive and read aloud.

Tell G I'm sorry. Maybe someday I'll come back. Dad, forgive . . .

The rest of the sentence was blotted, and only a sprawling *C* served as a signature.

The steady beat of hooves and a stentorian voice shouting, "Cyrus, Son, come back!" faded into eerie stillness. Naomi's lips trembled, and Judith burst out, "Thank God!" but the older woman finally cried, "God, have mercy on Elijah!"

Her own joy forgotten, Judith realized what this would mean to the stern father who had sacrificed his younger son to blind worship of the elder. Pity engulfed her and wiped away forever her anger at her father-in-law. The torment he had created for himself was punishment far beyond the laws of retribution.

Hours later, Lige returned alone. Joel lay asleep upstairs, but Naomi and Judith waited, huddled close to a blazing fire that seemed to offer little warmth.

"Was it Cyrus?" Naomi whispered.

"I don't know." Lige looked beaten, and Judith could not bear to gaze at him. The glazed eyes and the massive drooping shoulders showed more clearly than any cry of remorse the awful truth that lay ahead.

"Elijah, we must give thanks." Naomi stood and crossed to her tall husband. Judith could scarcely believe her eyes and ears. The woman who had sat crushed for hours grew in strength to meet the need. "Cyrus is alive. *Alive,* Elijah! All these months and years —" She faltered, then hope filled her face. "Don't you see? Our prayers have been answered!"

A ray of light penetrated Lige's despair, then died. "It is my fault," he said brokenly. "If I had been the kind of father I should have, Cyrus would have confessed openly." Misery returned to quench the hope. He crushed Naomi to him as if needing her physical presence, as if needing something to cling to while the world crashed around him. "And you, Judith, Daughter, your life ruined because of me. Oh, God, what have I done? Where are the sons You gave me? Cyrus, Gideon, forgive me!" He buried his face in Naomi's lap.

Judith's heart pounded. She ran to the man whose self-righteousness had caused such tragedy. "Lige, Naomi, Gideon is somewhere in Arizona. When Tomkins came last summer, he told me." She could feel bright color creeping into her face. "My life isn't ruined. *I love Gideon.* I realized it on our wedding day. Tomkins is coming back soon, and we're going west to find Gideon."

Lige raised his head. A trace of his old arrogance reared up. *"You aren't taking Joel!"*

"Yes, Lige, I am. He needs a father." Soft color mounted almost up to her coronet of braids. "I–I am sure Gideon loves me, and he will raise Joel as his own."

Lige's body went rigid, then he threw back his head and took a deep breath. "You are right, Child." He freed himself from Naomi's arms and shook himself as if coming out of a daze. "I drove my sons away. God won't allow me to destroy Joel."

Judith walked to him, took his heavy hand in her own, and gazed into his face. "Our God is a God of forgiveness. Gideon will only be glad you know the truth; I know that. You will be welcome in his home, with or without me, and Joel will always love you."

A little of the pain left Lige's eyes, but he left the room with the shambling steps of an old man who has outlived joy. Naomi ran after him and left Judith alone with the love she had openly confessed for the first time singing in her heart and in the still, spring air.

A few weeks later, Tomkins arrived. Lige Scott whitened but valiantly pulled himself together and welcomed the man who would be taking Judith and Joel with him.

"I haven't been able to find Gideon," Tomkins admitted, "but that's not surprising. Most of the messages I sent may never have reached Arizona. A man can't depend on riders who like as not take it in their heads to stop in Utah or New Mexico. We'll find him, and when we do, he's going to be one happy rancher." The miner's sally brought a blush to Judith's smooth cheeks. Yet her greatest joy came when Lige frankly told Gideon's faithful friend how he'd misjudged his son and pleaded for Tomkins to convince Gideon to forgive his father.

"Sho', he's already done that." Tomkins's hearty respect for a man who admitted his shortcomings showed in his lined face and relieved some of the suffering evident in Lige's brow. "That boy of yours is too big, or maybe it's his God that's too big, for him to hold a grudge. Better consider selling out here and heading for Arizona, Scott. Plenty of room there to leave behind troubles."

Judith saw the war that waged in Lige's heart, the leap of hope grounded by other considerations. "No, I need to stay here in case my older son comes back." The poignant admission brought tears to Judith's eyes, especially when Lige added, "Maybe someday."

"Gideon won't know me, will he, Judy?" Joel asked when she told him they were going to Arizona. "See how big I am?" He flexed his almost seven-year-old arm, and she pretended to find a muscle. "Can I take Millie? And my pony? Are Grandpa and Grandma going?" He hadn't lost his ability to ask questions.

"No, Dear. Millie needs to stay and take care of the Circle S. It's hundreds of miles, and we don't have a way to take her."

"Begging your pardon, Mrs. Scott, but there's no reason Millie can't ride along." Tomkins plunged into the conversation and received a gleeful hug from Joel. "The pony's getting too small for you, young feller. Besides, Gideon will have a real horse you can ride. I found some other folks who are heading west, so I up and bought a couple of covered wagons. We'll join with the band and be real pioneers." He cocked his head to one side. "You can take that pretty little pinto Patchwork if it's all right with the Scotts."

"Absolutely." Lige acted eager to co-operate. Judith could see the memory of his and Naomi's trek west long ago color his face and bring back life. "There's a trunk of Gideon's he might as well have, too, and my daughter will want to carry bolts of goods for clothing. Probably hard to get out there."

Judith's last sight of him was at the top of the mesa with Naomi, where she had dreamed so often. To her amazement, Tomkins had discovered that her towheaded friend Ben, who had first delivered her to the Circle S nearly three years before, longed passionately to go west and find Gideon. Now eighteen, strapping and cheery, he would drive Tomkins's second wagon.

Each day brought her closer to Arizona, closer to Gideon. If at times the thought crossed her mind he might have ridden on, she squashed it. God had worked in such incredible ways to bring them together, surely He wouldn't stop now. The dust and discomfort, storms, and threat of hostile Indians all became things she must endure.

Joel loved every minute of the long trip. He followed Ben around, rolled with Millie, and romped with others his age on the wagon train.

Some wagons turned off before the train went into Arizona. Other families saw places in New Mexico that attracted them. But Tomkins and his charges faced west, bound by a love for a young man who had captured their hearts with his sincerity and dedication. Always they asked if anyone knew of Gideon Scott. No one had heard of him until they reached Arizona.

"Gideon Scott. Hmm, name sounds famil'r," a frontiersman told them at Phoenix. He thought for a moment, his face in a dreadful scowl. Then it cleared. "Yup, he's the young feller that's set Arizony on its ear with his new-fangled idees. Won't 'low no drinkin' and ree-wards his cowpunchers by makin' them part owner of the Double J. Up near Flagstaff, he is." Dismay swept across his face. " 'Fraid I got bad news for you. He got shot up bad a few weeks ago. Can't say whether he made it. You kinfolk?"

"I'm his wife." Judith felt proud to say it out loud, and she managed to smile in spite of her stricken heart. They'd come so far.

Please, God, let Gideon be all right.

That night Joel echoed her prayer at their nightly worship they held regardless of where they camped. "God, take care of Gideon," the child prayed, his hand warm in Judith's, and together they finished with, "For Jesus' sake. Amen."

The new and strange country they traveled between Phoenix and Flagstaff brought wondering exclamations from Joel, whose gaze riveted on strangely formed cactus, red cliffs and canyons, and a host of other exciting things. Judith barely saw them. She resented the slow, steady pace of the mules that pulled the wagon, and her mind raced ahead of them, longing for the moment they would reach the Double J. The significance of the ranch's name beat into her brain and steadied her wildly beating heart when she wondered if Gideon would truly be glad she had come. As they passed through the huddle of buildings that made up Flagstaff and forged on, Tomkins muttered that they couldn't be that far from the Double J. Judith's pale face and haunted eyes urged him on, and Ben and Joel fell strangely silent. If their beloved Gideon had died, better to find it out at the ranch than from some wagging tongue in town. The hands would allow them to camp there, regardless.

■ ■ ■ ■

Why hasn't Judith answered Aldrich's letter?

The unanswered question pounded Gideon night and day. Yet days had limped into weeks that dragged by until spring slipped into the past and summer came. The doctor had been right. Gideon would always walk with a limp, and when he rode too long or too hard, his back hurt. A dream that had begun some time before of one day retracing his wild journey from El Paso to the Double J dimmed. He didn't know if he would ever be able to ride that far, even to carry the message of his Lord as he longed to do, then return to San Scipio and stay until he found Cyrus.

Sometimes he cried out to God, wondering if his father had intercepted the letter. Even though Lige believed him guilty of despicable behavior, he'd said Gideon could stay on the ranch. Surely he would respond if he knew his son lay dying.

Hope dwindled as time relentlessly rode on. More and more, Gideon relied on his heavenly Father for comfort. He would never be alone as long as the Lord traveled with him. There had to be a reason why no word came from Texas. Gideon's part was simply to trust God in all things, even when he didn't understand.

One afternoon Gideon sat astride Dainty Bess on a rise above the ranch house. Something white moved in the distance, dipped with the contour of the hills, re-appeared, and was followed by a second large white shape.

"Well, I'll be. Covered wagons!" Gideon curiously watched them, then said, "Gid-dap, Bess. Looks like we have company." He rode to meet the wagons, idly wonder-ing where these settlers planned to go. When, within good seeing distance, he discerned the face of the first wagon's driver, gladness filled his soul. *Tomkins?* Dainty Bess raced toward the billowing white wagon sail. She slid to a stop, and Gideon exploded from the saddle onto the ground to meet his old friend.

"You're a sight for sore eyes," Tomkins greeted and pounded him on the shoulder. "We heard you might be dead, and —"

A soft patter of feet interrupted him. "Gideon, you're alive." Judith ran straight to him, heedless of Tomkins's loud guffaw.

"You came." He stared at the white-faced girl clinging to his arm. "When you didn't answer Aldrich's letter . . ." He blinked to make sure she really stood there, travel stained as he had seen her so long ago, but beautiful and with a look in her dark eyes that repaid every heartache Gideon had experienced.

"I received no letter. Cyrus wrote and asked for forgiveness, but we were coming, anyway." Tears blotted out her incoherent explanation. "Oh, Gideon, God is so good." She raised her face to his.

He kissed the trembling lips and tasted salt. His arms circled her, never to let her go. "Judith, my wife." His heart overflowed. *"Thank God!"*

A second pair of arms surrounded him. He looked down. Joel's bright head rested against his jeans.

Later, there would be time to share the last weary years, Lige's remorse and repentance, and all that had separated them for so long. The silence in the sage had been broken. When storms threatened and howled above them, Judith and Gideon would face them together, united in love and blessed by faith in their heavenly Father.

The employees of Thorndike Press hope you have enjoyed this Large Print book. All our Thorndike, Wheeler, and Kennebec Large Print titles are designed for easy reading, and all our books are made to last. Other Thorndike Press Large Print books are available at your library, through selected bookstores, or directly from us.

For information about titles, please call:
  (800) 223-1244

or visit our Web site at:
  http://gale.cengage.com/thorndike

To share your comments, please write:
  Publisher
  Thorndike Press
  10 Water St., Suite 310
  Waterville, ME 04901